FISH CHANGE DIRECTION IN COLD WEATHER

FISH CHANGE DIRECTION IN COLD WEATHER

Pierre Szalowski

Translated from the French by
Alison Anderson

WINDSOR
PARAGON

First published 2012
by Canongate Books Ltd
This Large Print edition published 2013
by AudioGO Ltd
by arrangement with
Canongate Books Ltd

Hardcover   ISBN: 978 1 4713 4876 1
Softcover   ISBN: 978 1 4713 4877 8

British Library Cataloguing in Publication Data available

Printed and bound in Great Britain by
TJ International Ltd

For Antoni, Tom, Sophie.
For yesterday, today and always.

'In life, there is nothing to fear and everything to understand.'

Marie Curie

Nowhere and everywhere in Montreal

Thursday, 25 December 1997

CHRISTMAS GOES BY SO FAST

'Wait a little longer. Your dad's asleep.'

The clock said nine nineteen. I went and sat back down on the bed. I'd already been awake for two hours, waiting in my room. We have this family tradition. Every year Dad orders me not to show my face until after Santa Claus has come and gone. But I'm eleven years old and I stopped believing in Santa Claus five years ago already!

Five years, that's a secret; my parents think it's four.

I was six and a half when Alex, my only friend, came and told me the sad news with a big smile on his face. I was suddenly thrust into a world where there was an explanation for everything. To get over my disappointment, I did the same thing as Alex, at school. I got a kick out of telling the younger kids that Santa Claus was just something our parents made up. At home I dropped a few remarks to try and make Mum and Dad understand that it was about time they stopped telling me that if I wasn't a good boy Santa Claus wouldn't bring me anything. But when I saw the panicky look my mum gave my dad, I gave up trying. I didn't want to make them unhappy. Sometimes you have to lie to your parents to keep them happy.

'He's really cool, Santa Claus, because normally there's no way you can get an electric car that's a metre long to fit down the chimney!'

The following August, when I was out fishing with my dad at our summer cottage, I stared at the water for a long time.

3

'I don't believe in Santa Claus any more!'

He turned to look at me, and I turned to look at him. He stared at me for a minute, with a fatalistic little smile, then he put some bait on my fishing rod.

'That's life.'

Dad's not much of a one for talking. Mum says he's a man of few words. He came out with it as if he had known all along I would eventually find out, but he didn't want to be the one to tell me. He didn't try to find out who had told me, either, which you'd think would be instinctive for a policeman—well, former policeman. Now he was an instructor at the police academy. The doctor, who'd seen his fair share of brave folks, had diagnosed a mild case of burnout. What's so stressful about issuing parking tickets for the ladies who lunch on the rue Laurier! Besides, you shouldn't feel guilty, it's their husbands who pay, he'd said.

Mum says that the pressure comes from within. Only you can know why you're putting that kind of pressure on yourself, since you're the one who's doing it. My dad went on telling me bedtime stories anyway, about nice policemen who arrested naughty motorcyclists. Then one evening two years ago he quit. Every year, mid-January, my mum freaks out when the time comes for him to send his letter explaining why he doesn't want to go back to patrol work. *I don't enjoy it any more, and besides I get paid the same!*

After our fishing expedition, when we got back to the cottage, my dad whispered something in my mum's ear. She just pursed her lips. In her first grade class she'd seen plenty of kids who'd had to deal with learning the bitter truth about Santa

4

Claus:

'Why are you crying, sweetie?' she'd ask.

'My dad told me off 'cause I broke my Christmas present and he hadn't finished paying for it!'

But there in the cottage it was her own kid. Something had just ended forever. I'm an only child. Never again would she be able to play Santa Claus with my dad. That's when I realised that Christmas is as much about parents having fun as it is about kids.

*   *   *

Nine twenty-nine. Last night dinner went on forever. There were six of us around the table— me, my parents and Julien, my dad's best friend. Julien came with Alexandria and Alexandra, his unbearable twins. They screamed non-stop and since they look the same, it felt like it was always the same kid screaming. My mum was even more annoyed than I was.

'Alexandria! Alexandra!'

Then they linked arms and started dancing and singing. *'The sirens in the port of Alexandria, still sing the same melody . . . woo woo . . .'*

'Julien, couldn't you have given twin sisters different names?'

'Yeah, but then I would have had to have met their mum somewhere other than at a party devoted to Claude François and his song about Alexandria . . .' For the umpteenth time he was going to tell everyone about their names. 'Hey, and let me remind you . . .'

Every year Julien would explain that we didn't need to call them twin sisters, just twins, because

5

one twin is bound to be the sister of the other twin—provided they're both girls, of course; they mirror each other.

'Say, who's prettier?'

I could never tell which of the two pests was asking me this question. That was understandable as they were absolutely identical, so one or the other, same difference. The only good news was that Julien was divorced.

'I never wronged my wife, I just chose the wrong wife!'

So Alexandria and Alexandra sang the same melody only every other year. I never understood why he and his ex-wife didn't just share the twins. Since they had two just the same, they could each have taken one. But apparently twins can't live without each other. They're like parents, or my parents, anyway.

I wasn't supposed to know, but the twins had almost been my sisters. Julien was my mum's fiancé when they were both students at the teacher training college. Then he made the dumb move of introducing my mum to my dad, who was as handsome as they come, with his uniform hugging his abs, and his shoulders wider than his hips. He'd just joined the force. Love at first sight, she said. Dad said the same. As for Julien, he'd tried to mix business with displeasure.

'Hey Anne, hey Martin . . . I won't bother you any longer . . . Just stay there, I'll switch off the light!'

When the twins finally collapsed on the sofa in the living room, my mum came over and gave me a kiss.

'Bedtime . . .'

'But Mum, it's Christmas . . .'

'The sooner you go to bed, the quicker you'll have your presents in the morning!'

On the way to my bedroom I saw my dad and Julien opening another bottle. My mum wasn't there. Things looked serious because when I went by and waved to them, neither one gave me a smile. They even looked a little sad when they caught my eye. They must have drunk another bottle afterwards because when I woke up during the night to go for a wee they were still whispering in the living room.

Women fall in love because they think you're different. And then they do everything they can to make you just like everyone else . . .

*   *   *

Nine thirty-nine. *Knock-knock.* My mum opened my bedroom door. She looked in and she wasn't smiling.

'Your father is awake . . .'

I didn't jump out of bed the way I usually do on Christmas morning. I could hear the sadness in my mum's voice. At the time I didn't notice that she'd said 'father' instead of 'dad'. It was just her sadness that struck me.

When I left my bedroom I saw in the kitchen that it wasn't one more bottle my dad and Julien had drunk but two. Dad was waiting for me in the living room, slumped in his armchair in front of the television, which wasn't switched on, as if he'd made some sort of major concession for Christmas morning. He forced a smile and rubbed his head. I wondered if there were any other empty bottles

7

hiding out on the balcony.

Christmas may come only once a year but that's no reason to break with tradition. I was surprised my parents weren't sitting together. My mum wasn't perched on the arm of my dad's chair but on the sofa, further along. Separate.

Even when you're eleven, you always open the biggest present under the tree first. I knew at once that the chemistry kit was Mum's idea. She always buys me educational toys. For her a present should be useful. I'm a year ahead at school because she taught me to read when I was four. I was the star at daycare. Now I'm the bookworm who's a full head shorter than everyone else.

There were three presents left, almost all the same size. In this situation, you open the heaviest one next.

'This is Dad's little surprise . . .' He was staring at me.

I pretended not to see the dark look that Mum had just given him. I tore off the wrapping paper and my eyes popped out. Unbelievable! A video camera! I turned to my dad. All I could say was, 'Wow, Dad . . .'

He settled back in his chair, pleased. My mum clenched her jaw. I couldn't let her stay sad like that.

'Thanks, Mum, you too! Thank you, both of you . . . Thank you, Santa Claus!'

Her smile was strained. The video camera hadn't been her idea. I quickly opened the other two presents: first came a box of Lego, another of my mum's ideas, intended to help develop my fine motor skills. Actually, I'm so developed in that department that I can pretty much take a watch apart wearing a pair of hockey gloves.

The last package was a clock radio shaped like a football. It was from Julien. I'd told him last year that I was fed up with presents that had to do with baseball.

'But that Yankees bathrobe looks great on you!' he'd said.

I think he would have liked to have a boy. Maybe not two, but at least one of the two. Having to buy Barbie dolls in duplicate all the time must be frustrating for even the best dads. So he kind of made up for it with me.

'At least an alarm clock is more practical than a bathrobe . . .'

'You mustn't forget that it's not the present that counts, but the thought . . .'

I could tell my mum wasn't really talking to me, but to my dad. I went back to the box with the video camera. I sat on the floor with my back to them. I could sense that they didn't agree but, with such a beautiful toy in my hands, that didn't seem like my problem. I took out the instructions. My parents were whispering. I pretended to read, and I overheard everything, intentionally. I didn't know my mum knew how to swear.

'Shit, Martin. A thousand bucks for that camera! Don't you start playing that game.'

'He's been wanting one for a long time, and have you seen his report card?'

'He always has good report cards!'

'Aren't you the one who said we ought to encourage him?'

'If you buy him a camera when he's only eleven, how are you going to encourage him when he's sixteen? With a car?'

My mum got up and left the room. Hearing them argue because my present was too expensive made me sorry I didn't believe in Santa Claus any more. Especially since I had already heard way too many arguments this year. They almost always began with the same sentence: *Don't you ever feel like you're wasting your life, sitting there glued to the television?*

I turned to my dad. He was trying hard to smile. Then he stood up, slowly. No, very slowly.

'Urghh! My head!'

He went over to the bathroom. He tried to open the door but it was locked. *Knock-knock*!

'It's engaged!'

My mum shouted so loud that he put his hands over his ears. He came back and slumped into his armchair, almost embracing it with his body. Robot-like, he reached for the remote. Click. And on it went, the blahblah of the television.

It was nine fifty-nine on the news channel.

Christmas goes by so fast.

Sunday, 4 January 1998

THEY'RE ONLY KIDS!

Only three bulbs twinkled on a tiny string of Christmas lights on the tiny Christmas tree that stood on the coffee table next to two empty glasses and a bottle of wine that had breathed its last. On the sofa two cats nestled together, sleeping on a yellow shirt rolled up in a ball, its bottom buttons still done up. On the floor was a twisted pair of men's trousers, clearly removed in a great hurry. A short red dress lay carefully folded on the back of the sofa.

Along the hall, the bedroom door was ajar. In the dishevelled bed two shapes could be seen, both sound asleep. According to the clock radio it was two in the afternoon.

'Psst! Psst! Come on, here you go!'

In the kitchen, near a little flap at the bottom of the door to the balcony, a black kitten hesitated.

'Here, kitty kitty!'

The little creature took a step forward, crouched down and put its head through the flap. A hand outside, reaching up from the ground floor, encouraged the kitten, rolling a little red ball from left to right in the snow.

'Who's this ball for, hmm?'

The kitten seemed to think it just might be for him. For a moment he stayed poised. Yes, it must be his! He pounced. A hand grabbed him by the scruff of the neck. So it wasn't for him after all.

Meow!

On the sofa, deaf to the cry of distress from their kidnapped fellow creature, neither cat budged. The three little lights on the tree went on blinking. In the bedroom, one of the bodies had turned away from the other. A man's muscular arm emerged from the sheets to hang down the side of the bed, accidentally brushing the woman's back. She murmured something, then silence returned.

Ding-dong!

The man twitched, and sat up with a start. He looked around and in a panic he turned to the front door.

'Julie! Wake up!'

'Let me sleep . . .'

'There's someone at the door!'

'You're dreaming . . . Go back to sleep.'

Ding-dong!

The man ran frantically for his trousers, pulling them on even more hurriedly than he had removed them the night before. He bent over the sofa and quickly tugged at his yellow shirt. Two cats flew into the air for an instant before landing neatly on their paws. Buttoning his shirt, the man went to shake Julie.

'Does anyone know I'm here?'

Julie raised her head calmly.

'No one but me, the cats and you.'

The man looked hard at her for a second then turned, worried, to the two cats, who were purring innocently. Quite often a man is even more idiotic after lovemaking than he was before. Julie pushed back the sheet and got up. Her body was absolutely perfect. She headed into the bathroom, barely glancing at the man who was tucking his shirt into his trousers.

'You're married, is that it?'

The man pretended he hadn't heard, devoting

14

all his attention to zipping up his flies. Julie reappeared, wearing a short, red, faux-silk bathrobe.

'Luc, honey—that is your name, right, Luc? You've got a gift, I must say. Last night you were single, then one fuck with me and by morning you're married.'

Resigned, Julie pulled her bathrobe over her breasts. With a quick knot she cinched the belt around her waist, to keep the flimsy robe closed.

Ding-dong!

'Does your wife have a firearms permit?'

The moron seemed to have to think about that. Out in the hallway, Julie slid on a pair of high heels. Suddenly taller, she seemed even more slender, even more beautiful, even more perfect. From the way she walked it was clear she was used to perching on high heels. Her bottom swayed beneath the silky material. The man, terrified, hid behind the first thing he saw, a hat stand. His gaze followed Julie as she went to the front door. He might have made love to this gorgeous woman last night, but he wasn't looking at her bottom now. Julie planted herself firmly in front of the door, then opened it, unafraid. She knew she had done nothing wrong.

Meow!

There was the kitten, in the arms of a boy about twelve years old. Towering on her heels, Julie seemed disproportionately tall. The child's head came no higher than her breasts. Julie leaned down towards the cat in her young neighbour's arms. Her flimsy bathrobe gaped open slightly.

'Brutus! What are you doing out again?'

The boy's eyes zoomed in on Julie's half-naked breasts.

15

'He got out again!'

'That's the third time this week . . .'

Julie, who was well acquainted with the ways of men who look at women, immediately understood what her providential cat-rescuer was playing at. She leaned forward again and reached out for the kitten. Her bathrobe opened even further. The child didn't move. One of Julie's breasts was now almost completely bared.

'It'll catch cold . . .'

The boy, mesmerised by her hardening nipple, didn't budge.

'Alex, I'm talking about the cat. That's your name, right? Alex?'

'Yes, Julie.'

She leaned lower still to take Brutus. Alex, transfixed by the pair of breasts floating before him, practically touching his face, didn't seem to be able to let go of the kitten.

'Alex? It's not just the cat who'll catch cold . . .'

Meow!

Alex relented and handed Brutus to her, and the kitten immediately curled against his mistress's indubitably warmer chest.

'Thanks, Alex.'

'If he runs away again, I'll bring him back.'

Julie, amused, stared for a moment at the young boy: she liked his boldness.

'I'm sure you will!'

The door closed with a slam. Alex, proud as any prepubescent boy would be, turned to face the street. He raised his thumb with satisfaction— mission accomplished, victory! But still curious, he turned back to the glass in Julie's door, for a glimpse of her bottom disappearing down the

16

corridor. Suddenly he recoiled and rushed down the steps. He had seen the man.

'Who was that?'

'A young neighbour just brought Brutus back . . . Although I'm pretty sure he came for the view!'

'What?'

'He couldn't stop looking at my tits, is what I mean.'

'Well, there's definitely something to look at!'

The moron had reverted to type. Depending on what he expects from a woman, a guy can change all the time. Last night he'd played *Pretty Woman*, this morning it was *It Happened One Night* and just now, *Failure to Launch*.

'And did he pay, just now, to have a look?'

The look Julie gave him wasn't dark. It was pitch black. Blacker than black.

'And did you pay for last night? It cost you three dances, a bottle of wine from the corner shop and two hours of lying.'

To take a stripper home and get into her bed was the Holy Grail of the entire straight male population, the ultimate goal of a game where you bluff your way in, just like in poker. But the important thing at the end of the game is to slip in a harmless word, something to defuse the atmosphere as you leave the table, after you've cleaned up.

'Christ they start young these days!'

'Fuck off! They're only kids!'

FISH CHANGE DIRECTION IN COLD WEATHER

Four exotic fish, lit by a white neon light, were swimming in circles around an enormous aquarium set up right in the middle of the room. A plank set on two trestles was sagging beneath the weight of books on pure mathematics. Scattered over the books were sheets of paper covered in scribbled equations and obscure calculations. Other papers were strewn across the floor, some of them crumpled. In a corner was a sports bag bearing the logo of the Val-d'Or ice hockey team. Three hockey sticks had been set on top of it—sticks for a left-hander, with a very curved blade—an attacker's blade by the looks of it.

Across the street a door opened. Julie appeared on the ground floor landing, still wearing her very short bathrobe. She tossed an empty wine bottle disdainfully into the blue recycling box and it smashed. A man rushed out next to her, looking left and then right. He gave a slight wave that Julie did not return. She went in and slammed the door behind her. End of love story.

Boris Bogdanov had looked up from his reading—a book by Andreï Markov, not the hockey player but the great Russian mathematician. From his window he had seen everything. An enigmatic smile spread over Boris Bogdanov's face, as if he knew something his neighbour didn't.

Was Boris Bogdanov in love with his neighbour?

Nyet! Boris Bogdanov had never been in love, because in his entire life the only things that had ever interested him were himself and his fish. He had arrived from Russia in 1990 at the age of eighteen, dreaming of changing his life on the ice of Quebec's arenas. He was offered a chance to do just that, a spot at the beginning of the season at the training camp for the Foreurs de Val-d'Or in the Major Junior Hockey League. The recruiters thought this young Russian must be a rare pearl. And he'd fulfilled his promise, just not quite in the way that they'd expected.

Connoisseurs know that Russians don't like to play rough, but that they are very talented and born scorers. Boris Bogdanov had told the recruiters a few little lies about his past as a player for the Dynamo school club in Moscow; not big lies, just two dozen goals or so a year—half of them when his team was short-handed!

The first day of camp, during the rookie match, everyone quickly realised that he wasn't a real Russian player as far as his talent was concerned, but he was a real Russian player when it came to playing rough. During the first match, playing short-handed, Boris soon caught the attention of a big beefy player from Alberta who was out for his place in the sun. For this muscle-mountain, hard play was his meat and potatoes, the key to everything, the only corporal expression he was capable of. So this colossus did what all great predators do. He was a blue, so he looked at the backs of the reds for the weakest prey. The swiftest gazelle always gets away from the lion. For the slower ones, it's every gazelle for himself. And for the slowest of the slow, it's amen.

Boris Bogdanov never thought of playing the puck when it went into the corner. He was just

19

trying to get away from the enormous Albertan chasing after him. He heard him grunt. Boris wasn't as quick on his blades as he'd claimed. He didn't manage to get very far before there was a terrible *ker-runch!*

Boris Bogdanov, who was not all that hefty a guy, dislocated his shoulder when he hit the boards. All in all he had played only forty-five seconds in the Quebec Major Junior Hockey League, thirty-two of which were spent running away. In Val-d'Or, people like hard men, real men—but above all, they don't like being taken for fools.

'Don't count on us to pay for your ticket home!'

The equipment attendant did let him keep the hockey bag with the club's colours.

'A little souvenir for your kids.'

Just because you've told lies doesn't mean you're an idiot. The fact that Boris Bogdanov is an intellectual is proof of this. But it is a very intellectual stance to think that everyone else is an idiot.

If Boris did have a fault, that was it. He always went around with a little smirk on his face that meant he knew things others knew nothing about. He was a brilliant scholar and he knew it. Russians don't just make timid hockey players. They also make great mathematicians.

Boris Bogdanov was passionate about topology—about one of its disciplines anyway. Knot theory is a complex mathematical science that provides explanations for very simple things in life. When you pull on the yarn of a tangled-up ball of wool, sometimes it comes untangled right away, sometimes the knot gets even tighter. Life's just like that: little actions can have big repercussions.

20

And the same action doesn't always have the same effect.

Boris Bogdanov's exotic fish facilitated his research for a new theory. A fish in an aquarium always swims around the same course: that's the yarn. The fish unwinds its yarn according to the presence of other fish—friend or enemy—in the aquarium. Whenever a new inhabitant arrives, it must modify its usual path. For Boris, the trajectories of the fish were like so many threads, tangling and untangling.

'We don't choose our path, others choose it for us.'

His doctoral dissertation was there before him, in water maintained at a constant temperature of thirty-two degrees Celsius. This was vital. His academic survival depended on that water remaining at the same temperature. If it were to drop, some of the fish might change direction and thereby destroy the entire premise of his dissertation.

His research came to the attention of the President of the Mathematical Society of Canada, based in Calgary, Alberta, a very cold place.

'Come and see us when you've finished with your fish; for us it'll be a change from thermal mathematics!'

*   *   *

Through the window, Boris Bogdanov watched as his two young neighbours sat down on the steps outside the door to the building adjacent to Julie's. One of them was holding a video camera. Their eyes were glued to the tiny monitor. Boris turned

21

away from the window, put his book down on his untidy desk and with one finger dreamily stroked the wall of the aquarium. He could tell by touch alone that the water was at the right temperature.

*   *   *

Because fish change direction in cold weather.

THAT'S WHEN I UNDERSTOOD

'This is great! How do you rewind?'

'Let me do it, you're gonna break my video camera!'

'*Let me do it . . . You're gonna break my video camera . . .*'

'I'm not in the mood to mess around.'

'*Not in the mood to mess around . . .*Whatever! Take your video camera.'

Alex is like his dad, he always gets annoyed for no good reason. I don't hold it against him. It can't be easy to live with a single parent. When he was little, Alex used to say his mum was coming back. Now he never talks about it. It's a subject you avoid around friends who don't have a mum. It's not always easy, because among themselves kids talk about their parents a lot. The hardest time is Mother's Day. Then I avoid Alex. I wouldn't know what to say to him. He's easy to avoid then because he doesn't go outside. And no one knows whether he's heard from his mother because no one asks him.

'Why didn't you zoom? You can't see how the point got big—like *that*!'

I looked at the gap between his thumb and forefinger. Five centimetres! Only Alex would try and make you believe such a thing. At times like this, there's no point picking a quarrel with him. No matter how hard you try to show him he's wrong, he'll find an explanation for why he's right. It makes things really hard at school, especially with the teachers. The other reason for not picking a fight with Alex is that he is a full head taller than me, even if I'm only one year younger. He knows he can smash my face in, no sweat—I agree with him there. It's so obvious who's strong and who's weak, you can't do anything but stay friends. Alex gets in a fight at least once a week, on principle.

'Keeps you fit and it's good for your reputation!'

I have to confess I like Alex's reputation. Since everyone at school knows I'm his best friend, no one bugs me. With him arguments are always reduced to basics.

'First you hit, then you think!'

But while everyone at school has seen him hit, we have yet to see him think. In the school corridors everyone says he's crazy. And that he's proud of it. I know him, though, and he's not crazy, he's not proud—that's just his armour. Kids are cruel to each other. He just has to be even crueller. Death to anyone who teases him because he doesn't have a mum. Sometimes he gets good grades. Well, he would—when he can, he copies from me.

It was his idea that I should hide behind a car and film him while he was taking the kitten back to his neighbour. It was our third attempt. He was never satisfied with the result.

'Why didn't you zoom in on her tits?'

Two days earlier he had told me the angle was wrong. Four days earlier the neighbour came out fully clothed. The hard part was figuring out when she'd be in her bathrobe. She doesn't lead a normal life. She never gets up at the same time, and you never see what time she comes home. Summer's cool because she stays in her bathrobe for ages and she often goes to sunbathe on her balcony out at the back. Even my dad knows about it. I've seen him looking at her.

Alex gave me a friendly punch on the shoulder.

'I can't wait until tomorrow.'

He raised his chin. Just thinking about it made him happy. We looked down the street. The old guy who lives next door to us went out with his little dog. He lives with another guy who looks just like him, with very short white hair and a very long moustache.

'My dad doesn't like those guys.'

'Does he know them?'

'No.'

'Then why doesn't he like them?'

'Just doesn't.'

'They're brothers.'

'How do you know?'

'That's what my dad told me.'

'Has he ever arrested them?'

'My dad hasn't arrested anyone in a long time . . .'

Alex didn't look at me. That's the advantage of a kid with no mum. He doesn't want anyone asking him questions so he doesn't ask any either. The old guy disappeared around the corner. It was beginning to get dark.

'Hey, show me again!'

I rewound. We saw Julie open the door. It was incredible how you could see her breast when she bent down. Alex was especially interested in her nipples.

'Why didn't you zoom?'

If I didn't zoom it was because I liked seeing the whole breast better.

'What are you two still doing out?'

Even Alex jumped when he saw my dad standing

in front of us. I never knew I could switch my new video camera off so fast.

'What sort of nice things have you been filming?'

We didn't move. Alex turned to look at me, and I nodded. We must just keep quiet. After a while my dad understood he wasn't going to see anything. He turned towards our apartment.

'Is Mum home yet?'

'No, Dad, I haven't seen her.'

He looked around, worried. He rubbed his chin. You could tell he was wondering where she was. Then he started walking towards our door. He looked sad.

'Don't be long, the Christmas tree is waiting . . .'

'Coming, Dad.'

I got up and turned to Alex.

'See you tomorrow.'

He looked at my video camera. I could read his lips.

'Don't forget to bring it tomorrow . . .'

I winked at him and followed my dad. But I didn't leave Alex just because my dad was looking sad. Truth is, I love burning the Christmas tree. When I was little I would watch him do it. I had to wait till I was eight before he let me put the branches into the fire. They catch fire quickly, so it's true that it can be dangerous. It's really beautiful when the flame suddenly surrounds the dry needles. But the best thing of all is the sound. I never get tired of hearing that sharp crackling. Once the tree has burned and the decorations have been put away in the basement my mum serves the *galette des Rois*, the Kings' Cake. She's the one who started the tradition in our family. She found out about it during a trip to France when she was

26

younger and went there to study. Nowadays she makes the best *galettes* on earth. I love her almond filling. She puts in extra because she knows I love it. Then there's the bean. The one who gets it is the king or the queen. When you're king you get to choose your queen and if you're queen you choose your king. So every year my mum has been the queen.

'Where's Mum?'

'Out with friends.'

'Aren't you going too?'

'No, they're her friends.'

'What's she doing?'

'She had some things to take care of. She won't be long.'

My mum had things to take care of on *galette* day, the night before we go back to school? I didn't believe it for a second. I knew my dad was lying. There was something wrong with the situation. He noticed that I'd gone all thoughtful. I could feel his arm go round me, his hand on my shoulder. We stayed like that for a moment. Then we took turns putting tree branches into the fireplace.

'We make a good pair, don't we?'

'Dad, can I take my video camera to school tomorrow?'

'Out of the question! That's the ideal place to get it stolen.'

He looked at his watch and at the same time squeezed my shoulder even harder. He was worried.

Slam!

Mum was home at last. She was out of breath. My dad leaped up as if he'd been caught red-handed with his arm around me. In Mum's

27

hand was a flat white cardboard box.

'I didn't have time to make the *galette*. I stopped to get one at *Première Moisson*; they're the best in town. Smell that!'

I leaned over and sniffed the box. I should have said something like, *Mum, yours are the best in town!*

But I was angry at her for not making one.

'You're right, it does smell good.'

She seemed disappointed for a second. She smelled the box.

'Right. I'll heat it up.'

My dad followed her into the kitchen. I stayed by the fireplace. There were always a few branches that were still green, that had dodged the flames. I held them right up against the embers, one by one, mercilessly, so that none would survive.

'I'm not really in the mood to play the queen this evening!'

'It's not for us, it's for him.'

Gosh, my parents couldn't even be bothered to keep their voices down. I could hear everything.

'You're right.'

'And your apartment?' he asked.

'It's no good.'

'What do you mean, it's no good?'

'They're keeping it another month. The work on their new house isn't finished.'

'Where will you go?'

'Well, there's the cottage . . .'

'But how will you get to work?'

'I thought that maybe you could go to the cottage . . . Just for the first month . . .'

*   *   *

That's when I understood.

THEY LOVE EACH OTHER

It had been dark for a while by now. Boris Bogdanov watched from the window as Julie left her house. Beneath her half-buttoned winter coat she was wearing a very short skirt. The taxi had been waiting for a few minutes already. She quickly climbed in and the taxi sped away.

Boris Bogdanov sat down across from his aquarium and on a sheet of paper he carefully recorded the trajectory of one of his fish. His entire theory rested on his initial conviction. So before he could reach a hypothesis he must be sure his proof was well founded.

'*Da . . . da . . . da . . .*'

Research is very complicated, but the logic behind it is simple. Everything must be proved. If you maintain that Melanie can wee standing up, before you can prove that she wees standing up, first you have to prove that Melanie exists. If she doesn't exist, how can you maintain that she's having a wee? That is why Boris Bogdanov had to make sure, first and foremost, that his fish always swam in the same direction, over the same course. He had drawn the trajectories of each of his fish on a sheet of paper, using a different colour for each one. He ended up with an enormous four-coloured knot, and with this he hoped to prove that each fish's path depended on the paths of all the other fish.

Perhaps he should have paid more attention to Melanie having her wee. At least he could have had Melanie to talk to, because even with four fish it can seem really lonely when you feel like having a chat. The loneliness of the long-distance researcher.

*   *   *

There was classical music coming from the apartment across the way. Simon and Michel were sitting on their big sofa, luxuriating in the music. An LP was going round and round on a high-end stereo system. The interior design was tasteful, borderline rococo, with a dominant red note.

Before them on a little table was a bottle of Chivas Royal Salute 21 Year Old. Tonight, just like every night, they would drink two carefully measured glasses. The bottle lay in its blue velvet box, its neck adorned with a fine golden cord tied with a sailor's knot. At one hundred and fifty-nine dollars a bottle in the shop at the Rare Spirits Society, they took good care of it. An all-white Maltese bichon, 4 Year Old, was whimpering in her wicker basket.

'Simon took you out three hours ago. Patience, my friend!'

Simon and Michel had been living together for ten years, but they never went out together. It was as if they were in hiding. Everyone in the neighbourhood thought they were brothers. With their short-cropped white hair and elegant moustaches, they resembled each other a great deal.

They had met eleven years earlier. Simon was a psychoanalyst, and he had received Michel on his couch. Michel had gone into therapy for a malaise he could not explain. He was uncomfortable in his

31

role as father and husband. He loved his only son, who was eighteen; he loved his wife, and they had been married for twenty-five years, but deep down something was not right. He didn't feel well, as though he weren't really himself. Only his job at the weather office, Météo Canada, made him happy. He was a hurricane specialist, working on a matrix for predicting the precise path of these natural predators. Simon, too, was married, and had two daughters, sixteen and nineteen.

As time went by, they found they had things in common. Simon knew he must never get close to a patient. But the more Michel opened up to him, the more Simon understood him. They liked the same things. They began to wish they could share them. They simply felt good together. More and more, they felt unhappy if they spent too much time apart.

'Michel, I have two tickets for Alain Lefèvre with the Montreal Symphony Orchestra. I shouldn't normally go out with a patient, but it's at Place des Arts, it's not far from here . . .'

They went further than not far. Both got divorced at the same time and their families took it very badly. Particularly Simon's; he was Jewish. The psychologists' association of Quebec had never found out he was living with a former patient and they did not want it to get out. Whenever Simon took Pipo for a walk, Michel stayed home to cook. They had decided to keep their happiness to themselves, all the better to savour it.

The tempo of the music increased, from moderato to allegro. Simon's hand slid over to take Michel's.

*   *   *

32

They love each other.

AND I PRAYED TO THE SKY
TO HELP ME

My dad got the bean, my mum got the crown, I got nothing. They looked at each other. My dad breathed in, my mum breathed out a sigh.

'We have something to tell you.'

I didn't want to hear it, but on they went anyway.

'We want you to know that your mum and dad love each other very much.'

'Well . . . still love each other very much.'

'But, you know, sometimes you love someone, but everyday life gets hard . . . Things change . . . Time passes . . . You're not the same any more . . .'

This all sounded complicated. My mum paused to catch her breath and at the same time put the crown back on, which had slipped off her head.

'Sometimes it's so hard that you can't live together any more, because it's just not the way it used to be.'

Friends at school had told me how their parents had broken the news to them. I hardly listened to what came next; I'd already heard it.

'Your father and I have decided to split up.'

They stared at me, waiting for my reaction. I didn't move.

'We decided a month ago, but we didn't want to spoil Christmas for you.'

I lowered my eyes, so that I wouldn't have to say thank you. Let's not get carried away here. I didn't want to look at them, but I could tell they were looking at each other to see whose turn it was to speak. My mother has always been the more talkative one.

'You will still have a mummy and daddy, they just won't live together any more . . . One week you'll be with Daddy, here. The other week you'll come to my place. You'll see, it'll be almost the same as before. There are lots of children who are very happy living like this . . .'

That would make fourteen of us in the class now who migrated every week. Some of them say it's cool. I looked up. I was all churned up inside. My mum stared at me. I stared back. She seemed worried.

'Are you okay? You look like you're not bothered about this . . . You're allowed to feel something, you know.'

I had to say something. I didn't want them to imagine I didn't love them any more. I wasn't thinking straight.

'Who's going to cook when I'm at Dad's?'

My dad smiled as best he could. Not at all reassuring.

'I'm going to buy a cookbook, and we'll give it a go together. It'll be fun.'

It was off to a bad start, this shared custody business. I stood up.

'I have to get my bag ready for school.'

My mum just took my hand.

'If you need to talk, if you have any questions, you mustn't hesitate.'

I let go of her hand. She was expecting something. I went closer and hugged her. She squeezed even harder than me. When she let me go, I went and did the same with my dad. He squeezed me *really* hard.

'Dad, you're squashing me . . .'

I didn't have anything more to say or do. I went into the hall and headed for my room without stopping at the bathroom. I could hear them whispering. I didn't feel like listening to them any more.

In my room, once I'd closed the door, I felt weird. I heard them switch on the television. Off went my dad on his evening TV shift. My parents hadn't spoken for long and for once they hadn't argued.

I picked up my video camera but I wasn't in the mood to look at the neighbour's boobs. I rewound to New Year's. We'd spent it at Julien's place in Montérégie. I'd been spared the hyperactive twins jumping on the sofa. They were with their mum. It was better that way for Julien, he didn't have to run around after them all evening. Joint custody probably suited him. It only ever really suits the parents anyway.

I couldn't stop going back and forth between 1997 and 1998. I pressed rewind and listened to it over and over, the fateful countdown.

'Five . . . four . . . three . . . two . . . one . . . zero! Happy New Year!'

Then I saw my mum and dad wishing me *Happy New Year* into the lens. They'd had trouble finding the right words. Now I understood why they'd been so uncomfortable.

'Dad, get closer to Mum so I can see both of you in the picture!'

I pressed stop. I'd seen too much of them. I put the tape with the neighbour's boobs back in. I switched the video camera off and put it away in my schoolbag.

I stretched out on my back and looked at the

ceiling. It was white like before, but the white looked different. I didn't get it—everything seemed the same. But nothing was the same any more. Then it started, all of a sudden. Tears streaming from every corner of my eyes and pouring down my face. I put my hands on my cheeks but the tears kept coming. I couldn't stop them. I was crying as I'd never cried before. Usually I only cry if I hurt myself or a friend hits me. This time it was coming from inside. It hurts so much more. I didn't know that.

This couldn't be happening to me! Not me. How could they split up? Share me? Impossible! Your own parents aren't supposed to split up, only ever other people's.

'They mustn't! They mustn't! They mustn't!'

And I cried some more until there was nothing left. I didn't know that would end either. They hadn't even asked me what I thought. And yet it was my business too, it was my life! If they were behaving like this it must mean they didn't love me any more, since they had said they still loved each other, but not in the same way.

'Help me! Help me! Help me!'

No one answered. I was all alone. I went over to the window. It was raining, and I looked up at the sky, grey and black. I couldn't stop staring at it. I was so small, and it was so big.

*   *   *

And I prayed to the sky to help me.

BÉBÉ . . . JE T'AI, TOI, BÉBÉ . . .

'*Ten to twenty millimetres of rain, now that could cause a few problems* . . .' The man on the television screen was relaxed and in a cheerful mood. He strolled along through a light rain, in his loose green raincoat, doing his usual banter. Bad weather was his moment of glory. That was normal—he was the television weatherman. It went without saying that the sky held no secrets for him. He didn't give a damn there under his umbrella. The anchorwoman seemed to think it was pretty funny.

'Go and dry off! We want to see you again at the end of the programme. You must be completely frozen now!'

'He can go piss himself, that'll warm him up, fucking faggot.'

Alex didn't say anything. He didn't laugh. Or smile. In fact, he didn't even notice his dad's sarcasm. Ever since Doro—his wife, his love—had left him without warning, Alexis saw faggots everywhere. And when they weren't faggots, they were Jews, rarely both at the same time.

Alexis no longer looked at women and he didn't try to attract their attention. So no women were attracted to him. And yet at forty-five he was still a good-looking man . . . but he didn't like himself any more. Hating others was what kept him afloat.

'All fags! Fucking Jews!'

Around his son he was different. He had a gentle side, nurtured no doubt by his sense of guilt. Alex's hair was as black and frizzy as Alexis's was straight and fair and blondish-grey. Only their names were

38

similar. Just the kind of bad idea a dad would have.

'In Alexis, there's Alex!'

Every so often Alex asked Alexis to tell him who his mother was and why she'd gone away.

'I just can't, Alex. It's as if she no longer exists.'

It's not something you can talk about, a thing that doesn't exist. So Alex never asked again.

*   *   *

'What bullshit! They never told us yesterday that there'd be black ice, and now there is, and I'll bet you tomorrow there won't be any. Can you imagine, if I worked the way they do?'

Alex looked at his dad. It was at moments like this that he most missed having a mother. She was the one who should have been glaring defiantly at Alexis. She was the one who should be making him see reality, asking him, 'Would you look at yourself?'

Alex had often wondered if he'd really had a mother, if you could just come from nowhere. He had no memory of his early childhood. All he knew was that Alexis had been a musician, a singer-songwriter and guitar player. Alex remembered how when he was younger he used to spend long days at the recording studio. He could remember those huge mixing desks, and how he would sit sprawled on a sofa watching his dad behind the big pane of glass, his guitar strap over his shoulder. He may have been just a kid, and not meant to understand everything, but he had a fairly good idea what was happening.

'Alexis! It's always the same thing with you! Can't you just play what we asked you to play?

39

C minor is C minor, and A minor is A minor . . . And we're paying you to play C minor!'

'After a C minor you never play an F sharp, didn't your music teacher teach you that?'

'Alexis . . . All we're asking is for you to play the damn score, we don't give a fuck about your opinion.'

'No F sharps after a C minor!'

'You're impossible . . . Just get the hell out of here.'

'You don't know who you're losing! You'll be sorry!'

That was how the final sessions always went. Not one of the studios was ever sorry they'd lost Alexis. But he was blindly stubborn, so he didn't give up on his career. When you're sure you have talent, sure that you have the keys to success, you don't walk away from the profession that could turn you into a star. You just have to change direction.

'I'll make them understand what music really is!'

And so Alex followed his dad onto the streets of Old Montreal. Alexis busked, playing his guitar all hunched over, more mumbling than humming, as if he were only playing for himself and didn't care whether anyone heard him or not. When you don't have anyone to love, it's hard to sing love songs. Lovers would walk past him, give him nothing, then go and smooch on public benches. From that point on Alexis's condition deteriorated.

'All fags! Bleedin' Jews!'

*   *   *

So music had ditched him, too. But with a child to support, you have to eat. He began painting;

not pictures, but walls and windows, then ceilings, too. Everyone agreed he was a good worker. But too often he would forget to turn up, or he would quarrel with his co-workers, who couldn't stand listening to him any more.

'They're all fags, those carpenters! Fucking plumbers! Bloody Jews!'

It always took him a few days to get the feel of a new construction site. It was better for him to work on his own. Alexis was a drinker, of course. Not a chronic alcoholic, but at night he'd drink as many beers as he needed to get to sleep. The number varied.

When you've only got one person to love, and that person loves you, however badly, you love them back. Alex loved his dad. And he wondered why he'd been given this life. He knew his future was all plotted out. The educational director at school had said as much: *You'll come to a bad end, you will!*

Alex hadn't protested. He behaved the way all children do. It's not what parents say that matters, but the example they give. Looking at Alexis, no one could believe that his son had a happy fate in store.

'Night, Dad!'

'Are you going to bed already?'

'Got school tomorrow.'

'Already?'

'Yeah, Dad, it's the fifth of January, we go back to school.'

'You're too serious for your age.'

Alex wasn't serious at all. He fought with everyone. The shopkeeper at the corner shop didn't want to see him there any more, because he nicked things. Alex lied to his dad. He faked his signature. He copied his tests off his best friend. He never told his dad when there were parent–teacher meetings. And anyway, his dad was beyond caring about any of that. All he looked forward to was falling asleep on the sofa. First he snored, then he mumbled a song, always the same refrain.

'Bébé . . . Je t'ai, toi, bébé . . .'

Alex pulled a blanket over Alexis.

'Bébé . . . Je t'ai, toi, bébé . . .'

Alex never tired of hearing those gentle words. He often stayed next to his sleeping dad until late at night. It was so rare for him to hear anything about love.

*   *   *

'Bébé . . . Je t'ai, toi, bébé . . .'

Monday, 5 January 1998

'The forecast was for ten to fifteen millimetres of freezing rain, but we've got nearly double that amount: twenty-five millimetres in Montreal, thirty over the Laurentides and twenty in Montérégie. The weight of the ice has been affecting power lines, cables have started to break, and there have been reports of power cuts . . .'

YOUR PROBLEMS CAN'T BE THAT BAD

The alarm clock rang. I woke up with a start. I must not have been sleeping very soundly. For at least five seconds I felt really good. I stretched, and then it all came back. Happiness vanished. I got up and went over to the window and pulled open the curtain. The ground was shiny. Was that ice? I looked again. It was ice! I looked up and the sky was grey and ice was falling! Was this what the sky had done for me?

I ran into the kitchen, full of hope. My mum and dad were finishing their breakfast, staring into their mugs. When they raised their heads and saw me, I understood instantly that nothing had changed.

'Your father will be leaving today.'

I filled my cereal bowl and sat down across from them. But this morning I didn't feel like keeping silent in front of them, only to go and cry afterwards.

'I thought it was Dad who was supposed to stay here.'

I kept my tone cold, as if I didn't care. My mum, who knows me, spoke gently.

'The friend whose apartment I'm moving into was supposed to move into another place, but the renovations—'

'I know. They're not finished and that's why Dad is going to the cottage.'

They looked at each other. My mum made a face, my dad lowered his eyes. I didn't feel like being nice. I didn't like the fact they'd decided everything without me.

'Whose idea was it?'

'What idea?'

'To split up?'

They both had stupid looks on their faces. After all, as a rule, there's always one who does the leaving. They stared at each other for a long while. Judging by their expressions I could tell that if they didn't answer it was because both of them had had the idea.

'It's an amicable separation. We both feel the same way.'

They go and tell me they're splitting up, but they keep saying they agreed on it. When you agree with someone, it means you love them. And when you love someone, you stay together.

'And what if I don't feel the way you do?'

My dad was more surprised by my answer than Mum was. He looked at me as if he were seeing me for the first time. On the other hand, I could tell my mum was annoyed. She tried to stay gentle, but she didn't manage it.

'I realise this is making you unhappy, my darling, but these are problems between grown-ups. When a man and a woman decide to split up . . . That's life. It happens to a lot of people.'

'But there's three of us!'

My dad put his hand on my mum's. It was his turn to speak now.

'Your mother is right, it will be better for everyone.'

'But I'm better with both of you.'

'You'll still be happy.'

'I could be even happier.'

They should have just kept their mouths shut. I couldn't understand how they could say that to me. How could they imagine that I'd be happier without the two of them there together? I got the impression that they knew I was hurting, but they didn't want me to show it, so that they wouldn't feel bad. They were only thinking about themselves. As if it was all right for them to split up just because other people do. My dad got up and switched on the radio.

'Thousands of households in Quebec are without electricity, due to the freezing rain that has been falling for several hours . . .'

I spat my cereal back out. What was the sky doing now? I just wanted it to help me! I should never have counted on it. I stood up.

'I'm going to be late!'

My parents didn't say anything. They didn't feel like talking any more. I kissed them the way I had every morning, in my former life. I didn't want to start thinking that this was the last time I would have both of them there with me. It would only have set me off crying again. I just had time to overhear what my mother said as she was getting ready to leave.

'Give him time to digest the news . . . He has to find his own way through it.'

*   *   *

I rushed off to school. Well, not too fast, because it was really hard to stay on your feet. Alex was in a cheerful mood. He couldn't stop running ahead then sliding on the ice.

'My dad won't believe this when he wakes up.'

It's true, it was a strange sight. A fine layer of ice covered the ground. The cars looked like they'd

47

been wrapped in Cellophane, like sweets. An old lady coming out of the retirement home fell over right in front of us. Alex burst out laughing. I didn't laugh.

'It's not funny.'

'She didn't have far to fall, she didn't hurt herself . . . Look, she's getting back up. Or at least she's trying.'

'I should never have done it . . .'

Alex didn't know what I was talking about.

'Did you bring your video camera?'

I hesitated to tell him about my parents and the sky.

'If you didn't bring your video camera I'll be angry.'

'I have it, Alex, don't worry.'

'Shit, I can't wait to see it! It's going to be awesome!'

*   *   *

Someone who didn't think it was awesome was the educational director. There were at least ten of us gathered around the video camera. She couldn't see anything because the screen's so small, but she could hear all right. You couldn't help but hear. Everyone was shouting the same thing, and laughing.

'Show us her boobs!'

'Show us her boobs!'

'Show us her boobs!'

Eventually she saw them too. But it didn't make her laugh.

'Have you given any thought to this woman's dignity, while you go around showing her naked to

48

the entire school, and she isn't even aware of it?'

'You see lots of them on television, Miss, and besides, she doesn't know! We just won't tell her.'

Why make a fuss? The educational director looked up at the ceiling, sighing with exasperation.

'Only in secondary one and already a misogynist!'

She must have been one of those women who fight for respect and sexual equality for women, so she obviously didn't like Alex. She thought he'd come to a bad end, she'd already told him as much. She turned to me.

'But this isn't like you, not with parents like yours.'

The last thing I wanted was to let down my best friend, and I really didn't want to talk about my parents.

'Couldn't you find anything better to film?'

'No, Miss.'

'Why can't you be like a normal kid and film your friends, your parents, your pet . . . Make up a story . . . Free your creativity so that your inner child can blossom . . . But what you've done here is just disgusting! Poor woman . . . To think that even in this day and age we are reduced to this!'

Alex is never smart at times like this. Instead of doing what I did and looking down with a sad expression, to let the storm blow over, he started laughing like a moron.

'Whose stupid idea was it?'

She was on her feet, leaning against her desk, and she didn't take her eyes off Alex. I was wondering why she had asked, if she already knew the answer. Alex leaned forward, guilty no matter what.

'It wasn't him, Miss!' I cried.

49

The educational director was startled, and turned to face me. Alex looked at me too; he didn't know what was going on. Between us there had been a sort of pact: he may have been the one who dealt most of the blows, but he knew how to take a few as well.

'Yes, it was my idea, Miss.'

'Are you afraid of Alex?'

'No, Miss.'

'You mustn't be afraid here; you can speak the truth. If you've been a victim of intimidation, you have to tell me.'

'I'm telling you that it was my idea, Miss. I'm the one who talked him into it.'

Maybe that was going a little too far. Alex burst out laughing. He can never keep it in, especially when it's important. The educational director looked at us, trying to judge the situation. You could tell, even when he was sitting down, that Alex was a full head taller and at least fifteen kilos heavier than me. It was strange: there were three of us there and we all knew I was lying. She gave me a really nasty look.

'You want to play this little game with me?'

It wasn't that I wanted to play. I wanted to feel hurt, and then even more hurt. So that I'd stop feeling the hurt from my parents' separation. Alex looked at me. His eyes were telling me that he didn't mind taking the rap. He was used to it. But he didn't get it. I hadn't told him anything. The educational director started to walk back to her desk.

'Since that's the way it is, I'll ask your parents to come in. I'm warning you, you're risking a temporary suspension. Maybe they'll be able to tell

50

me who this is on the video. In the meantime the camera stays here.'

She sat down at her desk and picked up the phone. She pointed at Alex.

'What's your home number?'

'My dad's still asleep!'

'Oh, of course, how could I forget . . .'

She said it in a nasty way. Alex is a pretty tough kid, but you could tell it hurt him. Adults can be really mean when they don't understand a kid. She turned to me.

'Your number?'

'I don't remember.'

Alex looked at me as if he didn't recognise me. He'd always been the tough guy. Even I was wondering if I was still the same person. The educational director turned to a big bookshelf behind her.

'Since you think you're so smart . . .'

While she was looking up our numbers in her files, Alex edged closer to me. It was as if he didn't like me following the same path as him. In life you often prefer people who are the exact opposite of you. But for once we were both going to pay. I was waiting for it to start hurting.

Drrrring!

The educational director picked up the phone, but kept looking at us. You could see in her eyes that the hour of execution had only been postponed for the duration of a phone call. She was listening, and she looked annoyed. She turned towards the window.

'Oh? And it's not about to end? There's supposed to be more?'

She gazed at us, but she wasn't there any more.

'Oh dear, what a bad way to start the year!'

She hung up. She looked at my video camera for a moment, but it no longer seemed to interest her. It was as if she were lost, somehow. She picked up the phone—she needed help.

'Geneviève! Get on the PA system and make an announcement that the school will be closing at noon. The children who have permission to go home on their own can leave. As for the others, we'll have to call their parents, one by one. You take secondary one, two and five, I'll take three and four. Good luck!'

She hung up and looked at her watch, horrified at the thought of the hundreds of calls she had to make.

'It's going to take hours . . .'

We weren't surprised when she motioned to us to stand up. She shoved the video camera into one of her desk drawers. She didn't even look at us, just waved her hand as if to brush us away.

'Because of this wretched ice I don't have time to deal with your nonsense. Go back to class, and we'll talk about it tomorrow. Go on, out of here!'

In the corridor, Alex stared at me for a long time, still in shock.

'Was that lucky or what!'

'It wasn't luck.'

'I never have any luck, so for once when I do, believe me, I know what it is!'

'It's not luck . . .'

'I tell you, it was luck!'

'It's because of me.'

'It's not because of you, it's because of the ice.'

'And the ice is because of me.'

I had to lift my head because he was looking

down at me.

'How'd you do that?'

'I asked the sky to help me.'

'Asked the sky to help you . . . Is there something wrong with your brain?'

'Yeah, there's something wrong.'

He was still looking down at me, only not from quite as high.

'So why did you do that?'

'Problems with my parents . . .'

He wasn't looking down at me at all any more. As usual, he didn't ask any questions. He wanted to bring me back to my senses without hurting me. All it takes is one look to know what the other person is thinking. He put his hand on my shoulder, then he shook me gently, reassuringly.

*   *   *

'Hey man! Your problems can't be that bad.'

WHEN SHIT HAPPENS, HUMAN NATURE SHOWS ITS TRUE FACE

Boris Bogdanov was scared. He stared out of the window at the sky and then turned to look at his aquarium. He went out onto the kitchen balcony to check the electricity cables in the alleyway. They were sagging perilously under the weight of the ice. Would they hold?

He knew that without electricity he would not be able to keep his aquarium at a temperature of thirty-two degrees for very long. He went back to the sitting room and turned on the television.

'The forecast for this afternoon is for freezing rain. There is a chance of power cuts for Montreal and the entire region . . .'

Boris Bogdanov didn't want to hear any more. Click. He sat down across from his aquarium and stared at it for a long time, rubbing his chin, a sign that he was deep in thought. He bent down and picked up the first sheet of paper lying on the floor. One side was filled with calculations. The other side was blank. He grabbed a ruler and a pencil from the desk and quickly drew an isometric view of the aquarium. He measured its exact format. It took only a few calculations to work out the volume. For the likes of Boris Bogdanov, calculations like this are to a mathematician what hip-swivels are to a dancer: routine.

Then Boris Bogdanov went on to some thermal calculations. He drew a table and carefully noted the time it would take for the aquarium to cool, given the ambient temperature.

He was able to define an algorithm to determine the amount, and the temperature, of the water he would have to add to the aquarium if the temperature began to drop. If he removed one litre of water at thirty-one degrees, he would have to fill it with four hundred and fifty-nine millilitres at ninety-eight degrees for the entire aquarium to return to thirty-two degrees. He went on with his calculations, including the possible range of atmospheric pressure, if the water were to fall to twenty-nine, twenty-eight, twenty-seven, twenty-six, twenty-five, twenty-four, twenty-three, or twenty-two degrees. He didn't have the courage to imagine anything below that.

'*Nyet . . . Nyet . . . Nyet . . .*'

The excellent thing about Russians is that they know how to do without. Boris had lived in Russia for seventeen years. The first ten years of his life had coincided with the last decade of the communist regime. Doing without was something he was familiar with. But even better, like any Russian who's in deep shit, he knew how to get by in a precarious situation, in an emergency. Everything he needed was clearly stated in his list: a thermometer, a camping stove and as many canisters of gas as possible.

*　　　*　　　*

Boris Bogdanov was not alone in the aisles of Canada Dépôt, the giant home and garden supply centre. A lot of people were stocking up. People who'd already lost power mingled with people who might be about to lose it. And everyone was heading for the same shelves. Some were satisfied with certain bare essentials. Others, driven by fear, felt an irresistible need to stock up in massive quantities, even if that meant depriving their neighbours of *their* bare essentials. Boris Bogdanov completely emptied the shelf of little gas canisters. He took all the twenty-five they had in stock and rushed to the checkout.

*   *   *

When shit happens, human nature shows its true face.

I COULDN'T THINK OF ANYTHING
BETTER TO DO

As we walked down the street, Alex kept giving me looks. For him, that miraculous call the educational director had received was nothing more than pure luck. When the school emptied out, he just scratched his head. But I could see he was really blown away when the ambulance arrived at the school with its siren going. We were still there, so we saw everything. I have to admit I felt kind of bad to see the educational director flat out on her stomach on the stretcher. She was moaning and the paramedic was trying to comfort her.

'I just hope it's only a fracture, but by the sound of the pain you're in, I'm afraid you might have broken your coccyx.'

That was no comfort at all. She moaned even louder. She suddenly seemed so fragile, not at all the way she'd been in her office. Fortunately she didn't hear the students spreading the news. Everyone had forgotten that it was because she'd wanted to help sprinkle sand on the ice so that none of the children would slip and hurt themselves that she herself had slipped.

'The educational director broke her bum!'
'The educational director broke her bum!'
'The educational director broke her bum!'

Children are cruel, I know. Alex didn't say anything; he was too busy looking at me every five seconds. He was really puzzled, I could tell. We went home, not saying anything. The sky wasn't exactly helping me the way I wanted, but it had heard me, that much was obvious, which gave me hope. When we got to our street, I saw that my front door was open. A suitcase appeared, then another. My dad came next. Hope hadn't lasted long.

'What are you two doing here?'

'School's closed 'cause of the ice. Didn't you hear?'

'No, I haven't really had time to listen to the news this morning.'

I looked at my dad. I could see in his eyes that he really didn't want me there to witness his departure. In moments like these you just say what you can. He went first.

'I suppose you'll use the time to do your homework?'

'We didn't even have time to get any, Dad.'

'That's lucky . . .'

When he heard the word, Alex seemed to return to his senses. My dad grabbed his two suitcases.

'I have to get going, apparently it's pretty rough on the roads . . . Give Mum a kiss for me.'

Give Mum a kiss for him! He bent over me. I clung to him. I could see his hands squeezing the handles of the cases, so tightly they trembled. It can't be easy to leave. He hurried off to load the car, not looking at me—or rather, he didn't want me to see him. He started the engine right away. As he pulled out, the tyres skidded on the ice. He disappeared around the corner. Alex looked away.

'They're splitting up, huh?'

I didn't know what to say. Alex could tell I was holding back my tears. He was sorry he'd asked. He took a few steps back; even tough guys sometimes know how to be soft.

'I'm going home . . . That was awesome, your trick with the educational director. You're brilliant! The best!'

He said that to make me happy. He didn't believe a word of it. I think that in his shoes I wouldn't have believed it either.

When I got home, my mother wasn't there. So I spent the afternoon alone in my room, watching the ice come down.

*   *   *

I couldn't think of anything better to do.

IN LIFE, IT'S EVERY MAN FOR HIMSELF

Meow!

Brutus rubbed up against his lovely mistress's smoothly shaven calf. Julie was at her mirror putting on make-up. She didn't look either happy or unhappy, it was all just habit. It was a ritual to make herself beautiful, because it was her job to be beautiful. The Christmas tree had disappeared from the coffee table. Christmas was well and truly over. An hour earlier Julie had got a call from the owner of Sex Paradisio—he was expecting her at six p.m. sharp, ice or no ice. If she didn't show up, she shouldn't bother coming back.

'There's no such thing as winter in a strip club. There's only one season, and that's summer. Here it's hot indoors and hot on stage.'

Julie didn't even know why she went on doing this job. As a teenager she'd had a fierce desire for independence, and she'd been left pretty much to her own resources. She could simply have not run away, but love had found her for the first time when she met Max, a real smooth operator. She had just turned eighteen. He was thirty, and a sort of father figure. When he found out that Julie's savings account, which her grandparents had hitherto made impenetrable, had just been unlocked, he suggested they live together. The apartment was their little nest; they'd chosen it together. The lease was in Julie's name—Max didn't like to deal with paperwork. But he'd wanted them to have a joint account. She hadn't even finished decorating the apartment when Max disappeared, with every

60

dollar in the savings account.

'I'm just going to the corner shop for a packet of cigarettes. I've run out.'

Julie hadn't wanted to move. Not because of the memory of Max, but for the sake of her own independence. She didn't want a flatmate. At first she'd had to get a second job. She worked days in a restaurant, evenings at a bar. That's a lot, especially when you're working seven days a week. She'd had no time left to live. Chatting to one of her customers one night, he'd told her that she was far too beautiful to go on hiding behind a bar. He was the owner of Sex Paradisio. It hadn't taken him long to convince her she'd earn three times as much while working ten times less. He'd been telling the truth: when you're pretty, with big breasts, you've got a bright future in this field.

'You see that little bald guy over there? He sometimes blows three hundred bucks a night!'

Julie couldn't stop thinking about the future. She'd realised that being a stripper meant accepting that you didn't exist. The woman on stage unveiling herself to men's gazes, that wasn't her. And yet, even if it was some other woman who managed to earn up to five hundred dollars a night, it was Julie who deposited half of it every week into a savings account, in memory of her grandparents.

The owner of Sex Paradisio made a point of being tough with his girls, but he liked Julie. She behaved properly around him, but above all she behaved properly around the clients. Always smiling and friendly, a true professional. An example to her co-workers, who tended to be frivolous, their noses buried in powder, or hung up on second-class pimps—an even harder drug. With

61

Julie, everything was simple. That was why he'd called her, why he was sure she'd show up.

'If you don't show, you're fired!'

That was his managerial style, to threaten the girls. But he wasn't so crazy that he'd let Julie go, because she'd waste no time making one of his competitors happy. She'd promised herself she'd only do it for a while, but sometimes that *while* drags on too long. These days, she was just letting time go by, waiting for the right day to quit. Only love, the real kind, could make you quit a job that brings in five hundred dollars a night.

*   *   *

As she stood at her mirror, Julie suddenly grew four inches. She had just pulled on a pair of high-heeled boots. Brutus couldn't rub against her warm calf any more, and the leather was cold. He went to join his mates on the sofa. The larger of the two sleepy beasts made him understand with one swipe of the paw that he wasn't welcome, so he wandered around the house. There is a hierarchy among cats, too, and Brutus was still a long way from the top.

Julie came out of the bathroom wearing a superb, tight-fitting dress, all red, her favourite colour. She took her coat off the peg and put it on, and inspected herself one last time in the mirror, the one in the hallway this time. She opened the door.

'Bye, cats!'

Meow!

Brutus was the only one who replied. When you're at the top of the hierarchy, you often forget about those who helped you get there. Such is the

62

ingratitude of cats on sofas. It's often said they're independent. But they're merely using you, like men do, or at least like every man Julie had ever met.

'That's not a very good idea, Mademoiselle!'

Julie was startled. Even at five thirty in the afternoon, a woman alone is a woman alone. From her door she cast a suspicious look at the person who had just spoken, a man with a dog on a lead.

'I'm not sure those boots are the best thing to be wearing with what's coming down at the moment. Especially as they say it's going to last all night . . .'

'And who are you?'

'I'm your next door neighbour . . . and I work for Météo Canada.'

'I've never seen you around.'

'That could be because we're not on the same schedule . . .'

Julie didn't like the insinuation. Still wary, she walked down the steps to the entrance, forgetting to lock her door. One good look was enough to suss her neighbour out. She knew a ladies' man when she saw one, and he wasn't one. Her face immediately softened.

'So what's wrong with my shoes?'

'Your shoes look very nice, but I'm worried you'd fall even harder with them on . . . The emergency rooms are full of people who've slipped in the street. To see such a lovely woman lying in bed with her leg in a cast . . . That would be a waste!'

Julie smiled. It felt good to be in the presence of a man she need neither mistrust nor fear.

'Thing is I don't have any shoes without heels . . . I don't know how to walk without them . . .'

'I see. Well, if you're used to wearing them, just

don't take any unnecessary risks.'

The little Maltese bichon wagged his tail and came closer.

'And this is Pipo!'

Julie didn't even have time to smile. A taxi came tearing down the road. He was showing off, so he braked abruptly, only to skid foolishly on the ice. Taxis think the streets belong to them just because they know them better than anyone else does. But you're often in for a surprise when you think that way. *Bang!* Fortunately the rubbish bin he collided with was empty and, more to the point, plastic.

'I hope there won't be too much ice on your journey, otherwise you might be in for a pretty long ride . . .'

The driver, looking sheepish, got out and put the rubbish bin back in place, and Julie smiled. She bent down to stroke Pipo, who probably didn't get to enjoy a woman's touch very often.

'Nice meeting you. I'm Julie, by the way!'

'Michel . . .'

'It's really odd I've never seen you before . . . The dog looks familiar, but I don't remember seeing him with you.'

Michel clenched his jaw. He couldn't mention Simon, for fear of revealing their situation, and yet it was so obvious.

Beep! Beep!

The driver was in a rush to get back to his game of rubbish-bin skittles. Julie went back up the steps to lock the door to her little nest, then hurried back down and climbed into the taxi.

'I'll tread carefully, I promise!'

Michel watched the taxi take off in a zigzag across the ice. Once again, all he could think of was hiding. When Pipo lifted his leg for a final wee, Michel stared up at the windows of his apartment. The situation was becoming unbearable. He had to bring it up again with Simon.

*　　　*　　　*

Boris Bogdanov could have opened his window to tell his neighbour from across the way what he had just witnessed.

'Hey, your little cat has just got out!'

But he was not at all the sort you could count on. It might have meant going out and lending a hand trying to find the cat. Boris didn't want to leave his place, not even for a few minutes, in case the electricity suddenly got cut off. He turned to his aquarium. The four fish were still going around the exact same way. There on the floor, ready for an emergency, were a thermometer, a camping stove and only three little gas canisters . . .

*　　　*　　　*

At Canada Dépôt a customer had seen Boris emptying the shelves of gas canisters and had protested vehemently to the checkout clerk. Boris had maintained that he had the right to buy as many bottles of gas as he wanted.

'I'm a free Canadian!'

'Like hell you are! You can be a free Canadian all you want, but first you've got to show some solidarity with your fellow Quebeckers!'

A few customers applauded. People began to cluster around the source of this outpouring of wild, Russian despair, Boris alone against the

65

world. The manager came over to settle things in his best bombastic manner. Legally he had no right to stop Boris from buying as many gas canisters as he wanted, but under the circumstances, it was a matter of prestige, of corporate image. The very mission of Canada Dépôt was at stake. This was not the time to go telling his customers that business had never been better, that he had sold all his salt, all his ice picks, all his torches and every generator he had in stock, that he had tripled the order to be delivered tomorrow, and that he reckoned he would sell all of it in one day and beat his sales target, with a fine bonus to come.

'Young man, as the manager here, and given the forecast from the weather folks, I cannot allow this mass purchase. Come back tomorrow—I'm supposed to get more in. It'll be a pleasure to sell them to you.'

The manager of Canada Dépôt turned to his customers, and they all nodded approvingly. Normally they only came to him to complain, so he savoured this magical moment. Boris poured his heart out, but his Russian accent wasn't welcome on this day of great Quebecker solidarity. He told them about his fish and his knot theory, how vital it was to him. He took out his sheets of paper filled with complicated calculations to explain that with one gas canister, if the temperature fell to zero degrees in his apartment, he wouldn't be able to keep the water in the aquarium at thirty-two degrees for longer than one hour and thirty-three minutes. The manager waited for a moment before replying, to make sure all the customers were paying attention. Then he spoke very loudly.

'Sir, we're trying to help people here who've

lost their heat and who have children or old folks to look after who are going to suffer from the cold, and you want to take all the gas in the store for your fish? Why, that's a scandal!'

Thunderous applause from the customers. Aware that he was now centre stage, the manager took twenty-three of the twenty-five gas canisters from Boris's shopping trolley and carefully set them down by the till, as if they were the day's special offer.

'Anyone who needs gas can help themselves. But no more than two per person. Have a thought for other people!'

Shamefaced, Boris pushed his trolley up to the woman at the checkout. She picked up one canister to read the price. She multiplied it by two, then when she was sure no one was watching, she quickly grabbed a canister from the huge pile surrounding her till and slipped it discreetly into Boris's bag.

'I have fish, too. I know what it's like. It's a real can of worms if you don't look after them!'

Boris greeted this topological solidarity with a simple nod of his head, then hurried off to see if he'd fare better in another store. Unfortunately, the clientele of those other stores were all Quebeckers utterly lacking in solidarity. He couldn't find a single gas canister. The shelves were empty: other selfish shoppers had taken the lot.

Staring at his aquarium, Boris knew that if the ice storm led to a power cut, he would not last more than four hours and thirty minutes. So what if the neighbour's kitten had got out? With glacial indifference he watched Brutus scamper across the street. The kitten was lucky: a car went by but didn't run him over.

67

* * *

In life, it's every man for himself.

WHAT ON EARTH WAS THE SKY UP TO NOW?

When my mum came home, I threw my arms around her and gave her a kiss. I'd been doing a lot of thinking that afternoon. I couldn't let the sky do it all on its own.

'Help yourself and the heavens will help you.'

I don't know where I'd heard that phrase. But with all my thinking about the heavens, it came back to me. I hugged my mum as tight as I could so that she might think it was coming from someone else.

'This is from Dad!'

She stood there in my arms not knowing what to do. I wasn't trying to take revenge or hurt her, I just wanted her and Dad to understand that I existed, and if they thought they could just decide things without me, well, they were wrong.

'Did he get to the cottage all right?'

'Yes, he called. He said you saw each other before he left . . . They've had a heap of ice falling there, too, and the power is out . . .'

I froze for a second. I was almost ashamed to be in a nice warm house when my dad was cold. Served him right for leaving the house, but he didn't deserve to die frozen and all alone in the cottage.

'Don't worry, darling. He has everything he needs. You know him. He'll use the generator. The one he bought last year to do the renovations this summer, remember? The phone is working, so you can call him if you want, darling.'

'Later . . .'

'Whenever you want, darling. We're always here for you.'

Why was she calling me 'darling'? She never called me that. I have a name, after all! It really annoyed me, right from the start, and I didn't feel like being nice at a time like this. I had a plan.

'Will we go back there, to the cottage?'

'Of course we will, darling . . .'

I took a deep breath. She'd walked right into the trap.

'All of us together?'

By the look on her face, she hadn't seen it coming. I knew I'd hit home but I didn't care. I didn't want to tell her about helping myself. As for her, she really wasn't helping herself at all.

'Not necessarily, darling. The main thing is for you to have some good times together . . . And just think, dividing the time between your father and me will mean twice as many holidays at the cottage. You're one lucky boy!'

I just looked at her. She understood that I didn't think I was lucky at all. She closed her eyes for a second and came closer. I could feel her hands on my cheeks, ever so soft. She took her time.

'Forgive me, darling, I know this isn't easy for you. It's not any easier for me, for either of us. No one wants to have this happen, but that's life. Things will get better with time and besides, we're going to do everything we can to make it right for you. For your father and for me, you are the most important thing on earth.'

Thing! She's a teacher and that's all she could think of to say?

She kissed me tenderly. She seemed moved. I am sure she didn't go into the kitchen just to make

70

something for me to eat. I hoped she was crying, maybe not a lot, but a few tears at least. It was her turn now.

*   *   *

There was no answer. But I let it ring a long time. I redialled the number at the summer cottage and waited some more. My dad wasn't picking up. Where could he be?

'He must have gone somewhere to eat. It's hard to make dinner without electricity. Particularly when you don't know how to cook.'

My mum wanted to lighten the mood, but it didn't work with me. I could detect a certain amount of affection in her words, but knowing that my dad might not get enough to eat made me really sad. No child deserves this. We should have all been together, Dad in front of the television, Mum reading in the kitchen, and me somewhere in between. My mum wasn't relaxed. I think that for her too this situation wasn't as easy as she'd thought it was going to be. I was discovering what it meant to be a kid who's divided between two adults, and she was finding out what it meant to be half a parent.

My mum wanted to watch television. She sat on the armrest of my dad's chair. I don't know why—maybe deep down it was as if he were still here? Maybe she too would have liked him to be there with us, with the remote in his hand? Often the moments we miss the most are the ones we didn't especially enjoy at the time.

'At last I'll be able to choose the programme tonight!'

71

She chose the news channel, the one my dad always switched on first.

Could it be the sky was overdoing it, after all? All they could talk about was what it had been up to. My mum didn't like it one bit.

'Damned black ice . . . It sure picked the right time!'

All they were showing on television was the ice storm.

'You should film it. Think of the memories.'

'I don't really feel like remembering it . . .'

She grimaced, as if everything she said turned against her. But I could hardly come out and tell her that the video camera my dad had given me was in a desk drawer at school with a close-up of the neighbour's boobs stored on it.

'You know what? The educational director fell and broke her coccyx!'

'How'd she do that?'

'She slipped on the ice in the playground while she was sprinkling salt. She fell right on her behind.'

'Oh, poor woman, that must really hurt.'

*   *   *

In bed I thought about the educational director lying on her stomach in her hospital bed. Even if she was strict sometimes, I could remember all the times she'd been nice. Maybe she had kids who were sad to be at home without her. Maybe I'd really gone too far?

My mum came in to wish me good night. She sat on the edge of the bed and stroked my hair.

'Sleep well, darling . . .'

'Can I ask you a question?'

72

She'd had a rough evening. I can't say she seemed very enthusiastic.

'Of course, darling . . .'

'How did you and Dad first meet?'

She raised her eyes heavenwards.

'Oh, well . . . Listen, darling, maybe this isn't the best time . . .'

I put on my good little boy face, the one you use when you've just done something naughty, but not really very naughty.

'Oh, I don't know; give me time to digest all this. All right, darling?'

'Some other time?'

'Yes, some other time . . .'

She leaned down to kiss me.

'Don't read for too long, darling.'

She didn't wait for me to answer. She got to her feet quickly, afraid I might ask her another question. *Slam!*

When I switched off the light on the night table, I could hear the clicking of the ice falling against my windows. The sky had seen that I was trying to help myself, so it went on helping me. It felt good, knowing someone was thinking about me. I got up to look out of the window. The landscape was turning into something strange. The little tree across the way was bending under the weight of the ice, its top about to touch the ground.

I looked down the street: it was completely deserted. The light from the windows was reflected on the ground, in the ice. Suddenly there was a bright glow from the opposite side of the street. And then it was almost completely dark. The lights in the building across the way had all just gone out. I went over to my bedside lamp. Click. It came on.

73

*   *   *

What on earth was the sky up to now?

IT'S A MIRACLE!

The flame from the gas stove curled against the base of the aluminium saucepan. The water in the pan was boiling: one litre, no more, no less. Boris Bogdanov plunged a thermometer into the water and held it there with a trembling hand. The mercury rose slowly. The boiling water was beginning to burn his hand.

'*Crisse de marde!*'

That's how you can tell the landed immigrants— they swear in Québécois. Boris wasn't surprised to see the water boiling, once it reached a hundred degrees. That was something he'd learned in his second year at the Yuri Gagarin Primary School. He immediately extinguished the flame. He needed exactly a litre and, given the atmospheric pressure, he knew that the evaporation would be six centilitres a second. He only had ten seconds to transfer the liquid from saucepan to aquarium, because there, too, you can lose tenths of a degree.

Taking care not to burn any of his fish, Boris methodically poured the hot water into the aquarium. It took only nine seconds! He put the saucepan down and picked up the thick notepad where he had recorded the trajectories of each of his fish. His worried gaze moved in succession from each of his complicated drawings to each of his simple little fish. Suddenly the young Russian's face lit up. Not one of his fish had changed course!

'*Da ... Da ... Da ...*'

Boris's joy was short-lived. He looked at his gas canisters, then his watch. He got up and went over

75

to the bookshelf crammed with hundreds of books. He hunted for a moment and found a little battery-operated radio.

'No sign of improvement in the weather for Montreal and the South Shore, where the ice is continuing to fall. At the current rate of precipitation, we can expect roughly a million households in Quebec to be without electricity by tomorrow morning. Already several school districts have announced that schools will be closed tomorrow, and the same will apply to—'

Click. Boris Bogdanov didn't want to hear any more; it was clear enough. He knew that it was going to be a long, long night. He looked at his three gas canisters. A flash of hatred went through him, for Canada Dépôt, for the manager and for all those Quebecker customers with their damned solidarity. If the temperature of his aquarium started to drop significantly, years of work would all come to nothing. If his fish died he'd have to start all over again with his theory. For Boris Bogdanov this meant, incontestably, that he would have to establish the profiles of four new fish, which would require several weeks' observation for each one. Before he could prove that Melanie wees standing up, he would first have to prove all over again that Melanie exists. And he had four Melanies. He stood up and hurled the saucepan to the floor in a rage.

Crash bang!

*   *   *

'Fucking faggot up there! Can't we have five minutes' peace around here? Asshole!'

76

Yes, there had been some noise, but it was surely the first time the upstairs neighbour had made any. Alex had been listening to the news before going to bed. He dropped off to sleep in a pleasant cocoon, knowing that school would be closed the next day. He had taken an extra blanket in case the power cut lasted a while, and he put the other blanket on the sofa; he'd drape it over his dad later.

'Fucking weather report! They could've told us there'd be freezing rain! What am I supposed to do tomorrow?'

Alexis never did much of anything when tomorrow came.

'I'm going to call and tell them what I think of the way they do their job!'

He got up in the dark, not making the slightest move to pick up the phone, even though it was right there. He strode into the kitchen. With a firm hand he opened the fridge, which was very dark inside, and grabbed a bottle of beer. Then he closed the door and went out into the hallway.

Bang!

'What's all this stuff lying around, fuck!'

There was nothing lying around. It was just the doorframe. With one hand on his head he went haltingly back over to the sofa and lay down, pulling the blanket Alex had left over himself. He sucked on his beer to the last drop, like a baby. Then he lay on his stomach to forget everything, hoping he'd dream about Doro.

Boom ba-dah boom!

At three in the morning the sound of someone tearing down the stairs briefly masked the sound of Alexis's snoring. He was fast asleep, murmuring to himself.

'Je . . . t'ai . . . bébé . . .'

Then he rolled over into a foetal position, snoring even louder, and failed to notice that his son Alex had just tucked the blanket back round him. Outside, the ice was still falling. Then the sound of it on the window was drowned out by a sudden, heartrending, inhuman cry from the street.

'Neeeeeyyyetttt!'

Boris Bogdanov collapsed, theatrically, on the steps of his duplex. Ice was falling on his head, mingling with his tears.

'What have I done to God that this should happen to me?'

Boris Bogdanov did not believe in God, and he could not bring himself to accept an irrational explanation for the misfortune that had befallen him. For a mathematician, everything must be susceptible to proof. But he could not find an explanation for this ice. If it existed, it could only be God's fault.

Brutus couldn't understand what was happening, either. If he had only known, he would never have run away from home in the middle of winter, on a day of freezing rain. When he heard Boris moaning, he poked his head out from under the stairs and without a moment's hesitation jumped up onto Boris's lap. Boris didn't even try to push him off. He was weeping in a sort of rhythmic, monotonous chant, which made Brutus purr. A car door slammed.

The moment Julie's taxi pulled away she noticed the man lying on the steps of the house opposite, but in the dark she could not see who it was. She opened the door to her apartment and switched on the light in the hall. Warily, she turned around. She heard the weeping and gave a sigh of disgust.

'There's no point coming over here to cry, go back to your wife!'

Meow!

She raised her eyes heavenwards.

'Don't go trying the cat trick on me either. Leave that to the kids!'

Meow!

'Brutus?'

Meow!

'Right, give me back my cat!'

Julie saw that the man had not moved.

'Look, I'm tired, give me a break . . . No one showed up. I didn't even make a hundred bucks, and my patience is at the absolute limit.'

As she went closer she could see her kitten on the man's lap; his head was down and he was still weeping.

'Come on, give me Brutus, then go home and get some sleep!'

Boris, who had only just realised that Julie was speaking to him, looked up at last. Julie stopped short, feeling foolish.

'I'm sorry, I thought you were someone else . . .'

'I wish I were someone else.'

You never get men crying in strip clubs. In fact, Julie had never seen a man cry. She was always the one crying. She reached out for Brutus, but he stayed curled on Boris's lap, although Boris hadn't done anything to keep him there.

'It looks like he doesn't want to leave you on your own.'

'Is he yours? He must be cold.'

'Are you all right?'

'No, I'm not all right.'

'What's wrong? Did someone break your heart?'

'My fish are going to die . . .'

As he spoke, Boris could not suppress a huge sob. Although she did have a kind heart, Julie was flabbergasted that a man could cry over a bunch of fish.

'You really love them that much?'

For a moment Boris seemed to emerge from his sorrow. He grew thoughtful.

'Without them, my life will have no meaning.'

Broken hearts were Julie's speciality. She didn't know you could cry over a few fish but, in the end, the only real friends she had were her three cats.

'If you want, I can keep them at my place.'

'I can't leave them alone.'

Julie smiled: of course. Another girl trap.

'It's not what you think. The water mustn't drop below thirty-two degrees. I have to submit my dissertation in June. My knot theory is a mathematical revolution. I'm nearly there . . . I don't want to lose everything!'

Giving one last sniff, Boris Bogdanov dried his tears with the back of his hand and stared at Julie. He looked so pure, so honest. And even if his cheekbones were a bit too prominent, like all Slavs, he had a certain exotic charm. She'd never seen anyone like him at Sex Paradisio. She didn't understand a word he was saying about these mathematical fish. She just wanted to believe him, and hoped he wasn't lying to her.

'How many fish have you got?'

'Four little ones.'

'Is your aquarium very big?'

'It's average . . .'

'What's average, in your opinion?'

80

Boris Bogdanov merely spread his arms, removing roughly sixty centimetres from the actual length of his aquarium. Julie thought it seemed awfully small to accommodate four fish, but she was moved by her neighbour's unhappy situation.

'Just one night, then, because I'm expecting some guests soon. I warn you, you stay on the sofa and behave yourself. I'm armed and I've done three years of self-defence!'

Boris Bogdanov leaped to his feet. Brutus wasn't expecting this and went flying. Like any self-respecting cat he landed on his paws, but slid across the ice. He quickly steadied himself, then ran across the road and, without a meow, straight through the open door into his mistress's house. He was greeted by two unfriendly meows: he was still not welcome on the sofa.

Julie didn't even have time to demonstrate a single self-defence movement: leaping to his feet, Boris Bogdanov threw himself on her and embraced her in a manly, very Slavic manner, patting her warmly on the back as if he would never stop.

'All right, fine, I see you're happy . . . Go on! Go and get your fish.'

Boris bounded up the steps to his place four at a time and went straight to the sitting room. He stared for a moment at his four fish, swimming in pairs. He plunged the thermometer into the water: twenty-three degrees! Not only did his fish risk forgetting their trajectories forever, they were now bound for the great beyond, even as they continued to weave their knots. He had to save them!

Boris spread his arms to pick up the aquarium. It wouldn't budge an inch. There was far too much water in it, and too many stones at the bottom. He grabbed the saucepan and dipped it in the aquarium, then ran to empty it in the toilet. After a few trips he faced the bitter truth that this manoeuvre would take hours. At this rate his four little treasures would end up frozen. There was only one thing left to do. He grabbed his fishing net.

*   *   *

Boom ba-dah boom! on the stairs.

Still sprawled on the sofa, lost in a dream, Alexis didn't budge. Alex was sitting on the floor with his back against the bed, enjoying every moment.

'*Je . . . t'ai . . . bébé . . .*'

Boris Bogdanov pounded on Julie's door. It had taken him over half an hour to catch his four fish. In any group there's always one that doesn't want to follow the others. When Julie opened the door, she was wearing her red bathrobe, the collar carefully wrapped high around her neck. She had just got out of bed.

'I didn't think you were going to come after all!'

She saw the saucepan in Boris's hand and the four fish wiggling around in a terrible knot.

'That's very kind of you but I've had dinner already.'

Boris Bogdanov had never had much of a sense of humour, and even less so in the presence of his four little treasures who were swimming their hearts out in their iron coffin.

'Can I see your bathroom?'

'Dream on . . .'

'It's for the fish!'

Julie felt a bit sheepish. She pointed down the

82

hallway. Without a glance or a thank you, Boris Bogdanov ran to it and locked himself in. *Slam!* Julie opened a cupboard and took out a blanket, which she left on the sofa, careful not to disturb the two cats sleeping there. Then she went up to the bathroom door.

'I've left a blanket for you on the sofa. Don't think you can sleep anywhere else, otherwise you'll wake up in the emergency room!'

'*Da!* Thank you very much!'

'The towels are under the sink.'

'*Da!* Thank you very much!'

'Where are your fish?'

'They're here with me.'

'Can I see them? They were all on top of each other in the saucepan.'

'*Nyet!* I'm too busy!'

Astonished, Julie reached for the doorknob. She thought for a moment of turning it and going in without warning. This was her house, after all. But this intrusion, so totally unexpected and unlike anything she'd ever experienced, was a change from her usual routine. It was about life, and where there's life, there's hope. She went to her bedroom and looked out of the window at the falling ice. Yes, the ice storm had completely emptied Sex Paradisio, something unheard of in that world of men who love girls, but she wasn't sorry. There were other things in life besides money.

*　　　*　　　*

Day was breaking and Julie hadn't managed to get to sleep. From the bathroom there came a continuous sound of water running, then stopping,

83

then running again. For the first thirty minutes or so she figured it must be the unexpected, unique nature of the event that was keeping her awake. There was something of a lullaby about it. But even the sweetest refrains, if they're repeated too often, will get stuck in your head and become unbearable.

'It's time to calm this mathematician down!'

Forgetting to put on her bathrobe, Julie rushed into the hallway, wearing nothing but her fine, see-through nightie. She flung open the bathroom door without knocking. This was her house, after all!

'Now you and your fish, you are going—'

'*Shh!*'

Boris accompanied his command by putting his finger to his lips. Without knowing why, Julie obeyed. He was on his knees facing the bath, surrounded by flannels and scribbled sheets of papers strewn everywhere, and he motioned to her to come closer. She froze for an instant. Her short nightie wasn't hiding a thing. Boris wasn't looking at her, though.

'Come and see, in the bath.'

Julie obediently knelt down. From behind, the scene was one of torrid indecency. Julie's bare buttocks bounced next to Boris's worn jeans. When she leaned forward to peer into the water, her breasts nearly burst out of the thin material of the nightie—but Boris did not notice a thing, preoccupied as he was with his makeshift aquarium. At the bottom of the bath where the plug should have been there was a face flannel. One hundred and nineteen centilitres drained through the cloth per minute. By maintaining a fine trickle of water from the tap at forty-two degrees, at a steady volume, Boris had succeeded in the incredible challenge of keeping the temperature of the water at a constant thirty-two degrees.

'It's all written on here!'

Julie took the sheet the Russian genius handed to her, but she hardly looked at it. Thermal equations, with face flannels thrown in, weren't really her thing. But she did marvel at the sight of the fish swimming in her bath. It was one of the most beautiful things she'd seen in a long time. Even Brutus thought it was a pretty sight. He'd managed to jump up on the sink to watch the aquatic performance. Julie pointed to one of the fish.

'What's his name, the green one with orange stripes?'

'Number One.'

Boris paid no attention to her bare leg as he reached under her knee for a little pad of paper. He turned back to the bath, flipped over a few pages and stopped at a drawing where the basic trajectories of each of the fish were pencilled in different colours. He pointed to the path drawn in green and dotted with orange.

'That's him!'

Leaning into the bath, his face practically in the water, Boris followed Number One's progression for a long time. Then he turned to the trajectories of Number Two and Number Three. He finished with a meticulous observation of Number Four. He placed his hands against the edge of the bath to push himself up. Julie turned to him. He did the same, his eyes popping out, and instinctively she covered her breasts. He quickly turned back to the water.

85

'Look! Look! They're all on track again!'

Boris grabbed Julie's bare shoulders with his manly hands. He shook them unrestrainedly, causing his charming hostess's breasts to bounce so vigorously that a wardrobe malfunction nearly ensued. But she let him shake her—he wasn't even looking that way. His big blue eyes were staring intensely at her face.

* * *

'It's a miracle!'

Tuesday, 6 January 1998

'At noon several pylons in the region of Drummondville collapsed beneath the weight of the ice. Now in Montreal up to seven hundred thousand households are without power. The Red Cross has set up its first emergency shelters. The forecast is for continued bouts of freezing rain. This weather has already broken a number of records.'

CAN THINGS LIKE THIS REALLY HAPPEN?

'Don't tell them you did it, otherwise they'll strangle you!'

A Hydro-Québec truck had just stopped in front of us. The two men in the cab, their eyes red, their faces drawn, were eating a sandwich while they looked at the long list of places they still had to go to. It started me thinking. Not Alex, though.

'You see that? With their messy hair they look like Gremlins!'

Maybe they had kids who were sad they couldn't be with them. Maybe their wives had made dinner but they didn't have time to go home. I remembered the images I'd seen on the news at noon. They showed these enormous electricity pylons collapsing under the weight of the ice. *'It is unlikely that the situation will improve, since freezing rain has been forecast for the entire day tomorrow. Nearly seven hundred thousand households are now without power . . .'*

Including my dad. He had called that morning to tell us about his day, but mainly to inform us that the generator was holding up.

'But you should see the way it guzzles gas. I had to go to the gas station twice!'

He was not the only one going to fill up his jerry can for his generator. The gas station manager had had to step in. People were shoving, squabbling.

'No more than twenty litres per person!'

Then my dad told us how these two Hells Angels showed up on their bikes, in spite of the icy roads. They weren't afraid of anything, but everyone was

89

afraid of them, especially the manager.

'Twenty cans of twenty litres? Sure, no problem, I understand your plants have to keep warm to grow!'

Dad didn't tell them he was with the police.

'There were two of them. I was all on my own, with nothing more than a jerry can for a weapon . . . An empty one, to boot.'

After my dad hung up, my mum didn't really try and talk to me. I think the discussion the night before had tired her out a bit.

'I have so much homework to correct!'

This was good timing. It meant I could go and meet Alex. He told me about his night without power. I could have taken him to our place, just so that he could have a shower, but I was a coward. I didn't want him to see my new life. And besides, he didn't ask for a shower.

'You know that guy upstairs from me, he goes over to the neighbour's to get laid.'

'You're kidding!'

'He was making so much noise up there that he woke me up.'

'If he was making noise upstairs, then he was upstairs, not across the way.'

'I saw him go into her place with a saucepan.'

'A saucepan?'

'He made some little dish for her.'

'In the middle of the night?'

'It's not the main course that matters, it's the dessert!'

'The dessert?'

'Well yeah, the dessert, that's when you get into bed, after you've had dinner . . .'

I don't like talking about that stuff.

'At least he got to sleep in a warm place!'

I'd noticed Alex's uncombed hair, that crumpled look people have when they've slept in their clothes. He looked at me. He could tell I was embarrassed and I guessed he was about to make fun of me.

'I was thinking that with your magical powers maybe you could do something. I don't feel like being cold tonight . . .'

I didn't know what to say.

'Are you our young neighbour who lives opposite?'

We both jumped. One of the brothers was standing there, looking at Alex.

'Yes, sir.'

'My name's Simon. Michel and I live across the street from you. We heard the power is out on your side of the street. There was some noise last night in the flat next door and we figured out that that nice young lady let your upstairs neighbour stay at her place. He's Russian, or so I've heard . . .'

Simon had this grown-up smile on his face, convinced we didn't know what he meant. They must have had one huge dessert.

'What's your name?'

'Alex.'

'Alex my boy, tell your dad we have a spare room to put you up in. Michel works for Météo Canada. This is going to last a while, kids. The situation is getting worse.'

Alex pointed at me. Was he going to tell him that it was all my fault?

'So why does he have electricity?'

'Because he's lucky and lives on the same side as we do. We're on the same grid as the old people's

91

home next door. We live in a priority zone.'

Alex turned to me, stunned.

'You really thought of everything . . .'

'Tell your dad that you're both welcome.'

'Thank you, sir, I'll tell him . . . But he's kind of anti-social.'

'Tell him he can feel right at home.'

'He's not that sort of person . . .'

'In a situation like this it's perfectly normal to lend a hand. When the heavens won't help, we have to help each other. Right?'

I took this as a reproach. But if he were in my shoes, he might understand that there are times when you have to act to get what you want. I clenched my jaw. Then he opened the door to his place.

'We'll be waiting for you. Come whenever you like. I insist! You're more than welcome.'

Slam! The door closed. Alex turned and looked at me for a really, really long time. I knew he was beginning to change his mind.

*   *   *

'Can things like this really happen?'

WHAT A BEAUTIFUL THING, A MAN WHO SAYS HE'LL BE BACK

Julie was in bed, her hair dishevelled, and she was finding it hard to open her eyes. It was already three o'clock in the afternoon. Her head was aching. How had she got into such a state? Then it all came back to her: the Russian, the bath, the face flannels, the additions and subtractions and multiplications, the fish . . .

*   *   *

'We have to drink a toast!'
   'What, now?'
   'Do you have something to drink?'
   'An old bottle of tequila . . .'
   'Davai!'
   Since she was still in her nightie, Julie thought he must want to get her drunk to take advantage of her, and he lost all the gold stars he'd acquired so far. She slipped quickly into her red bathrobe. And as for Boris, the tequila slipped down his throat, more than once. After a while, it was doing the same with Julie. Boris sat on the floor, his back against the bath. She had been hesitant to join him there, so she was sitting on the toilet. The alcohol had loosened their tongues.
   'Mathematics is poetry. Every line, every formula rhymes with the one that follows, and makes a long, beautiful poem. A mathematical formula is a work of art. A text you write only once, and you mustn't make any mistakes, so that it becomes unique!'

93

'That's lovely, the way you talk about it . . .'

Boris Bogdanov turned and looked at Julie for the first time. His gaze lingered. She smiled. A researcher always feels that he must convince the entire world, that he must wage a terrible battle in utter solitude for a cause that he alone understands. Boris was not used to being in good company. He raised his empty glass.

'*Davai!*'

'Last one . . . It might make you lose control of your calculations.'

Boris gave a fleeting smile. Russians, whether they are researchers or hockey players, think of each drink as nothing more than a port of call on the way to the next glass. The main thing is to forget everything, to let yourself go and, above all, never to stop.

'And what do you do in life?'

'I work in a sort of, um, amusement park.'

'For children?'

'No, for adults, really.'

'Do you enjoy it?'

'It depends on the evening . . .'

'Why?'

'You come home late, it's crowded, you catch cold easily, people come for a good time but they're not always nice.'

'So why do you go on working at this amusement park?'

'I intend to stop, soon—I don't know yet.'

'What would you like to do after that?'

'I've never thought about it.'

Boris unscrewed the metal cap on the tequila bottle. Julie was annoyed with her reply. It really didn't look too clever to go telling a researcher that you didn't think about things. To fill the silence, she held out her little glass stamped Absolut Vodka in blue, a gift from a spirits rep who'd had no money on him to pay for the last dance. She wanted four of them, and he'd said okay. She had danced for him, but he only gave her two. The glass reminded Boris of his country.

'Since we have vodka glasses, I'll show you how we drink in Russia.'

He filled two glasses then held his arm out to Julie. She thought he wanted to chink glasses, but he came closer, on his knees, and wrapped his arm through hers. Then he lifted the glass to his lips. She did the same. Tangled together in this simplest of knots they raised the Mexican liquor to their lips, trying very hard to pretend it was vodka. Boris paused and stared at Julie, whose pink cheeks already betrayed that she'd been drinking . . . and perhaps something more than that.

'*Na zdorovye!*'

'*Na ndorovye!*'

'No! *Na zdorovye!*'

'*Na zdorovye!*'

In a single gulp Boris swallowed his glassful of tequila. He breathed out, long and slow. His breath, suddenly Mexican, encouraged Julie. She threw her head back and emptied her glass in one go, then tossed it over her shoulder. *Smash!* It shattered against the wall.

'Why'd you do that?'

'Well, it's tradition.'

'It's only in American films that Russians smash their glasses. Given the number of litres we drink, in such a poor country we can't afford to break so many glasses!'

95

Julie didn't want a diplomatic incident, especially since, with the exception of *From Russia with Love*, she didn't know a thing about Russian cinema. Boris patted the floor and Julie finally came to sit next to him.

'We'll take turns.'

He filled the glass, handed it to her, and she drank. He filled the glass again, didn't hand it to her, and knocked it back. The process was repeated three times without a word until Julie brought up the fish again.

'Why are you making all those calculations with your fish?'

'I want to prove, in a mathematical fashion, with a topological theory—hence the knots—that we do not choose our path, but that others choose it for us.'

'Do you really need all those calculations to prove that?'

'What do you mean?'

'Take me, for example. Other people always decide my life for me . . .'

A long silence settled over them. Boris turned to Julie, who suddenly seemed very sad. Alcohol can be conjugated in every tense, including the imperfect, and melancholy is a necessary stage on the way to alcoholic nirvana. Boris began to sing in Russian. Even though she did not understand a word, Julie burst into tears. It sounded so sad. It was going to be a long night.

*　　　*　　　*

'It's three o'clock in the afternoon already!'

Julie emerged from her bedroom with a terrible

96

headache and a persistent bitter taste in her mouth. On the sofa in the sitting room the two cats slept, undisturbed. A knot, a little one, formed in her stomach.

'Don't tell me he's left, too?'

She opened the door to the bathroom, lifted up her nightie, sat on the toilet and closed her eyes. She tried to remember where she had last seen her Russian mathematician. She opened her eyes again and there on the floor beside her she saw a pair of legs. Still leaning against the bath, one finger in the water to check the temperature, Boris Bogdanov was sound asleep. Brutus lay on his lap, purring. In the corner, the tequila bottle had gasped its last.

Julie, while doing what she had come to do, looked around her, relieved. This was a good way to start the day. She'd met her fair share of men and plenty of them had come to her place. And in the morning, waking up next to them, she would see them for who they really were. But this one lying here before her was not like the others. He hadn't even tried to follow her into her bedroom. Yet she wouldn't have refused him.

Julie stood up, climbed over what remained of her Russian evacuee, and looked at the fish for a long time. When Boris began to snore, she leaned forward. Her eyes were glittering with desire. Slowly she began to remove her nightie . . .

*   *   *

'*Aaaaaaaahhhhh!*'

Boris had been ready for anything, but not this! Neither had Brutus.

When he raised his heavy head and turned

towards the bath, he almost passed out. Julie smiled at him. He immediately leaned over to see where his fish were. Perfectly peacefully, in water at thirty-two degrees, they were mapping out their paths.

'This morning I noticed that it's as if they haven't realised that the bath is bigger than the aquarium. They don't use all the space. So I sat down just here where they don't go.'

Sceptical, Boris observed his fish. He leaned forward and followed Number Two as it swerved less than ten centimetres from Julie's naked breasts. Number Three did the same, and Number Four, too. When Number One swam towards her left breast, Boris leaned right down to the water. The orange fish with the green stripes also continued on its way without the slightest regard for the enormous sphere in its field of vision. Boris did the same. Either way, Julie had not even bothered to cover her breasts, convinced as she was that this man was unique—the only man she had ever met who could actually dress her with his eyes.

'Da . . . Da . . . Da . . .'

Boris raised his head and turned to the little mermaid. Julie could not help but shiver. In his gaze there was something she had never had the good fortune to enjoy: respect.

'A magnificent observation.'

Julie thought of hugging Boris to thank him for his compliment, but she *was* naked. Besides, Boris was already on his feet, looking at his watch. He pointed to the fish.

'They memorised the space and volume of the aquarium, but I don't know how long it will last . . . Can I trust you with them, just for the time it will take me to go and get it?'

She just looked at him. He stared back for a moment, seemed to hesitate briefly, then, won over by her frank gaze, he capitulated.

'I'll be back!'

Boris went out without saying goodbye. That was something Julie was used to. All the same, an indefinable smile lit up her face. A tear slipped gently from her eye, then another. She did not try to wipe them away.

*   *   *

What a beautiful thing, a man who says he'll be back.

THEY'LL BE FINE HERE!

'They could've warned us. I swear they're all fags at the weather office!'

'My dear Alexis, you don't know how right you are ...'

Michel, petrified, looked down at his plate. He loved Simon for his gift of witty repartee, but in this case he had surpassed himself. Alexis felt encouraged.

'Besides, I wonder if they're not all Jews to boot!'

Michel closed his eyes to pray. He turned worriedly to Simon. Alex sensed there was something weird going on. Only Simon didn't seem the least bit fazed.

'What makes you think that, Alexis?'

'If it's not one, it's the other.'

Simon watched as his guest took his time helping himself to a nice slice of roast. He noticed that he was shovelling the shallots to one side. Simon didn't like shallots either.

'You work at home, I suppose, since you seem to be there all the time?'

'At the moment there's not much on, what with this ice.'

'The ice started yesterday, Dad.'

The symphony of forks lasted a good while. Alexis could sense everyone staring at him.

'Is that any of your business, Alex?'

He didn't say it in a nasty way, but to be given a home truth in public—that was just not on. Alexis appealed to Michel and Simon as witnesses.

'It's true though, isn't it! Since when do kids

get to stick their noses into grown-ups' business? He still hasn't got it into his head that over the Christmas holidays there's not much call for renovation!'

Alexis had no sense of time passing: he hadn't noticed that Alex had grown up. Now he wolfed down another slice of roast, chewing energetically, oblivious to basic etiquette that dictated that you shouldn't speak with your mouth full.

'And what sort of work do you do?'

'I'm a psychoanalyst . . .'

'Ouch! Better watch what I say, huh?'

'It's pretty rare for people to come and see me just to watch what they say . . .'

'And you?'

'I work at Météo Canada.'

The piece of roast went no further. When you talk with your mouth full, that's the risk you take. Alex, Simon and Michel all looked over at Alexis who, with great difficulty, managed to swallow his lump of partially chewed meat.

'It wasn't you I was referring to, just now . . .'

'If you'd known, you wouldn't have said it, naturally . . .'

Alexis looked down into his lap. If he could have hidden under his slice of roast he would have. Simon smiled mysteriously. A psychoanalyst is like a professor or a policeman, he can never leave his profession to one side.

'And you, Alex my boy, how are things at school?'

'Well, these days it's pretty quiet—'

'Cause of the ice!'

Pleased with his joke, Alexis chewed the next bite of roast with a wide smile. A little moment

101

of contentment wafted over the room. Oddly enough, Alexis felt good in this unfamiliar place, with these people he had only just met and whom he had thought he would despise. He had to find something nice to say.

'Thanks for having us over.'

'It's only natural.'

'What with the other fag upstairs who didn't stop dancing all night . . .'

'You mean that young Russian student from next door?'

'Is he Russian?'

'Yes, I think so. But yesterday it was more like he was studying Québécois . . .'

'I don't mean to contradict you, my dear Michel, but it was more like he was studying young women from Quebec.'

At the end of the meal, Alexis scratched his forehead. He hesitated for a moment, then ploughed ahead.

'Alex told me you guys were brothers.'

'In a way . . .'

'Huh?'

'Do you like whisky?'

'With Coke, yeah.'

'I mean *good* whisky.'

'With good Coke, yeah.'

'This is not the sort of whisky you mix, my dear Alexis . . . Have a walk around the apartment while I get things ready.'

Michel was pacing nervously around the kitchen. Had Simon lost his senses? The whole point of settling in this humdrum neighbourhood all those years ago had been so that they could remain discreet. Simon went up to him.

102

'Have you seen what you've dragged in?'

Simon put his arm around Michel reassuringly.

'Calm down, my love, the situation is under control.'

'You can't control an idiot like that!'

'He's not an idiot, he's just not very well . . .'

'He's sick, I agree! And he'll go and tell everyone.'

'He won't say anything to anyone . . . At least, not for the time being.'

Michel was still nervous. Simon caressed his cheek.

'He's no more homophobic than you or I.'

'Well, you wouldn't know it by the sound of him.'

'Calm down, Michel . . .'

Eeek! The floorboards creaked. Michel instinctively drew away from Simon. Alex was looking at them from the kitchen door. In this sort of situation, only a false cough will do. Michel volunteered.

'*Ahem, hem.* A little walk with the dog?'

'Uh, sure, yeah, sure . . .'

'Pipo, where are you, you naughty little Pipo?'

Once he was sure that Michel and Alex had finally gone out, Simon brought out the bottle of Chivas Royal Salute 21 Year Old, and set it down on the little coffee table in the sitting room. He removed the precious bottle from its velvet case. He turned the stopper. He filled only two of the three glasses. He heard footsteps walking around the apartment. He sank deep into the armchair to wait, serene. Alexis, puzzled, came to sit on the sofa opposite the armchair.

'Is this a sofabed?'

'No.'

'Oh? Well there's something I can't quite figure out here . . .'

'Tell me.'

'I saw there are two bedrooms and a study where there's no bed, so I just wondered where we're gonna sleep?'

'In the room down the hall.'

'But then where do you sleep?'

'In that room there.'

'And your . . . brother?'

'In that room there.'

'Huh? But it's the same room.'

'Michel, who is not my brother, sleeps in the same room as me because we always sleep together. Like any couple.'

Alexis narrowed his eyes. Simon handed him a glass of Chivas Royal Salute 21 Year Old. *Glug!*

'You're not really supposed to drink it all in one go . . .'

Alexis opened his eyes and stared at Simon for a long time. He put the empty glass back down on the table.

'Sorry . . .'

'No need to apologise. There's some left. The bottle is half full or half empty. It all depends on how you look at it. How do you see it?'

'Completely empty.'

Simon nodded, a connoisseur of couch confessions.

'Tell me, Alexis. Are you afraid of black people?'

'No, why?'

'You never get angry at them?'

'No, never!'

'If I tell you my name is Simon Birnbaum and that I'm Jewish, is it a problem for you?'

'Well no, not any more . . .'

'You know why, "not any more"?'

'No.'

'Because you've identified me.'

'Huh?'

'What you are afraid of, Alexis, is people you cannot identify—homosexuals, Jews . . . A black man, you can see he's black, you're not afraid of him. Now that you've spoken with me, and you have an idea who I am, the fact that I'm a homosexual, and Jewish as well, doesn't bother you, or doesn't bother you . . . any more, shall we say. You need something to mark the difference. You weren't born like this, Alexis; I know you certainly weren't like this before. But before *what*, do you know?'

Alexis shuddered. The memory of what he did not want to talk about any more was there again. When something hurts, even if what you've just heard is very complicated, it feels good to find yourself in the presence of someone who can help. Alexis had, through a simple glance, asked for help. He was aware of what he had become. He just didn't know how to get out of it. He let himself sink into the soft couch, head back. Simon poured him a second glass of Chivas Royal Salute 21 Year Old.

'If you like, you can put your feet up on the table. You should feel comfortable. Just mind the whisky bottle, if you would . . .'

Alexis, docile, stretched out his legs and set them gently on the little table, careful not to touch the bottle. Simon crossed his hands on his lap.

'Alexis? Tell me about your childhood . . .'

Alexis took a tiny swallow of whisky. He kept it in his mouth so that his taste buds would absorb all the different flavours. He set the glass down in front of him, took a deep breath, and set off on a journey back in time, starting deep inside himself.

*   *   *

'Roll over!'

Out in the street, Alex burst out laughing. He couldn't stop.

'How does he do that?'

Pipo, following Michel's twirling hand, was rolling over on the ice. The moment his master stopped waving his hand, he lay still, wagging his tail.

'How did he learn that?'

'We're not too sure whether he taught us or we taught him.'

'I think you taught him.'

'Sometimes animals have something inside them already and all we do is discover it. Like with human beings.'

Alex could tell that Michel was trying to get some message across, like 'the world is a beautiful place'. He didn't want to hear it. It reminded him of the ethics classes they had at school.

'What else does he know how to do?'

Michel snapped his fingers. Pipo began to crawl.

'Can I try?'

'Try, it might work. It depends on him.'

Alex snapped his fingers. Pipo crawled.

'Roll over!'

Pipo rolled over on the ground to the rhythm of Alex's hand. Alex was flabbergasted that the little dog had obeyed him.

'Does he do it with everybody?'

'No!'

Alex couldn't get over it. As a boy-on-his-way-to-a-bad-end, it felt good to know that he could do something that no one else could do. But every victory has its price.

'Now you have to reward him.'

'What do I say?'

'You stroke him and tell him you're pleased with him. All he wants to do is please you.'

Alex stroked Pipo, who rolled over on his back.

'Now he's surrendering; you've become his friend, he trusts you.'

'That quickly?'

'It's instinctive.'

Just for a moment, Alex thought that maybe the world could be a beautiful place. This was nothing like his ethics classes, where it was all just theory. He smiled at Michel. That was a nice thing he'd just said. He went on stroking Pipo.

*   *   *

'Gently, I said!'

Boris Bogdanov had never learned how to shout quietly.

'You mustn't break it!'

'Do you always get stressed out like this?'

Careful not to slip, Boris and Julie were carrying the aquarium from the dark apartment over to the little nest opposite. Boris hadn't been able to carry it on his own. As she turned, Julie saw Michel, Alex and Pipo, who was still on his back.

'So now it's Michel's dog you've found?'

She gave him her little smiling wink, no hard feelings, but Alex still blushed bright red.

'Gently!'

107

'Yes, yes, I heard you, gently!'

'Well, Julie, he certainly seems to know what he wants!'

'I'm not too sure what he really wants.'

'Don't worry, when the ice melts, everything will go back to normal.'

Julie's smile faded and she almost slipped in her high heels. She knew one thing, she preferred this abnormal everything. Hadn't she already stuck her neck out by telling her boss at Sex Paradisio that she wouldn't be coming into work that night?

'I'm sheltering four fish and a Russian!' she had told him.

'I already told you not to go getting cosy with the mafia.'

'He's not mafia, he's into knots.'

'Don't you take me for a fool, Julie, the mafia is everything but slipknots. I don't like you hanging around with Russians. You want me to tell you what they do to women?'

'This one doesn't do anything to women! Not a thing! He just makes knots with his fish. He's got no power and no heat. I can't let him stay there on his own. It's just for a day or two. Show some solidarity!'

'I'll tell you where to put your solidarity—you're fired! That's not how we work over here at Sex Paradisio!'

True, solidarity wasn't exactly Sex Paradisio's stock-in-trade. Among the girls it was every woman for herself, and stealing each other's clients was the very definition of team spirit on high heels.

Julie hadn't felt a thing, getting sacked like that. The only thing that surprised her was that every time she met someone new, in other words practically every evening, she always told them up front that she had no intention of quitting her job. Men are like that: they desire you because you're a stripper, but the minute you sleep with them, they want you to stop stripping, and they don't want other men looking at you. Julie didn't have a relationship with Boris yet, but she'd already grown used to the idea that she wouldn't be stripping any more. She'd been giving it some thought.

'Let's put it on the table in the sitting room, because of the cats.'

'Wherever you like, Boris. Wherever you like.'

*   *   *

'They'll be fine here!'

STOP IT, YOU'RE HURTING ME!

If it weren't for the ice, Alex wouldn't be playing with the neighbour's dog, and our Russian wouldn't be moving in with the most beautiful girl in the neighbourhood. I moved away from the window. There was nothing left to see. Why wasn't anything happening to *me*? Maybe something was going on elsewhere. At the cottage, my dad picked up the phone right away.

'Have you got heat?'

'Course.'

'So you're not cold?'

'Course not, I've got the generator. It's not a big one, but it does the job. Well, that is, if I can get gas tomorrow . . .'

'And what are you eating?'

'I've learned how to make a ham sandwich.'

I'd run out of questions.

'And how are things at home?'

'Okay. Mum's on the computer. She's doing some calculating.'

'Yes, I know.'

'Are you going to work tomorrow?'

'No, all the schools are closed, even police school.'

'What are you going to do?'

'I'm going to try and get the ice off the roof, there's way too much on it right now.'

'Aren't you afraid you'll slip?'

'I'll be careful, I promise. And what are you going to do tomorrow?'

'I don't know.'

'Have you been using your video camera?'

'I'm afraid I'll slip and break it.'

'I hope you're being nice to Mum.'

I could tell my mum must have told him what I'd said the night before. It must have hurt her. I wanted to apologise. He spoke first.

'Seems you were feeling kind of down, or so she said . . .'

'I'm pretty bored.'

'It's this damned ice that makes everything complicated. Things will go back to normal afterwards.'

I'd run out of strength to talk. I felt guilty and my eyes filled with tears. I didn't want the ice to complicate things, I wanted it to fix them. It wasn't doing any of the things I had asked. Why had I even bothered?

I went into the big storage room that we used as a study. My mum was typing slowly on the computer keyboard. When she saw me she suddenly stopped and with a click she closed the document on the screen. I just had time to see it was an Excel spreadsheet. They'd started teaching us Excel at school two months earlier.

'Are you okay, Mum?'

'Yes, darling.'

'What are you doing?'

'Sort of . . . bookkeeping.'

'Can I watch television?'

'Do what you like, darling, you can even stay up late, there's no school tomorrow.'

'Thanks, my sweet Mummy!'

I hugged her. She was surprised at me clinging to her like that. I didn't feel like helping myself any more. I'd been mean enough the night before.

111

What was the point of making her cry? I love my mother. In the end, hurting other people doesn't make you feel any better. And besides, it didn't do any good. What I was trying to do was just too hard. Children can't decide things, I should have realised that right from the start. There's not a thing you can do once your parents have decided to split up.

'I love you so much, sweetheart. Right! Go and watch television.'

Hugging her did her good: she seemed relieved. I was throwing in the towel. Split up, share me between you, I won't say another word.

I curled up in my dad's spot, in 'his' armchair with 'his' remote. Before was before. I had to stop hoping he'd come back and that life would go on just like it used to. I surfed through all the channels. On Le Canal Nouvelles all they talked about was the ice. It was perfect for them. But the problem with these non-stop news programmes is that they end up repeating themselves. I heard the same thing over and over again so often that for a laugh—well, actually in order not to cry—I started multiplying. Seven hundred thousand households without electricity times the number of evacuation centres, add a thousand volunteers and multiply by twenty-five millimetres of ice: what do you get?

'The cost of the storm could be devastating. Damage is already estimated in the tens of millions of dollars . . . And the ice has not stopped falling . . .'

I was ashamed of what I'd done. If it had solved my problem, I wouldn't have minded, but . . . it was all for nothing. I ran towards my room, angry, but before I got there I stopped suddenly in the storage room.

112

'Night, Mum.'

She wasn't there. My gaze landed on the tray by the printer. On the bookkeeping sheet there were two columns, 'you' and 'me', and loads of numbers. I read, 'video camera: one thousand dollars'. In the 'you' column was written, 'five hundred dollars'. Same thing in the 'me' column. There was a comment in the margin: 'we were still together . . .'

It's the thought that counts, not the present . . . Easy to say.

Everything in the house was listed. I saw that my dad could keep the electronics but he had to give up the sofa and his precious leather armchair. What? The sofa was worth three thousand dollars? My dad was keeping the television, six hundred dollars, but giving up the computer, eight hundred. There was a line marked 'alimony: five hundred dollars'. It was spread over a year. It looked like my dad wouldn't be paying anything until April because my mum was getting the big double bed and the big dresser in the sitting room, which came to two thousand dollars. And in the middle of all those figures, there I was like a piece of furniture. Hardly worth any more than the sofa.

I heard the toilet flush. I rushed to my bedroom before my mum was even out of the bathroom. *Slam!*

The sky hadn't done a thing for me; on the contrary, my situation was getting worse by the day, by the hour. I went to the window. I stared at the sky and shouted.

'Stop it, you're hurting me!'

Wednesday, 7 January 1998

'Contrary to all expectations, the storm has begun to lessen in intensity. Hundreds of Hydro-Québec team workers have been busy repairing and replacing poles, power lines and damaged pylons. Three hundred thousand users have already been reconnected to the grid. Everything would seem to indicate that the situation will soon be under control.'

BUSINESS IS BUSINESS

The first thing Julie saw when she woke up was the Hydro-Québec trucks doing a waltz. It was nine o'clock in the morning. She hadn't woken up this early in ages. She went into the sitting room: there was absolutely no doubt about it, this was no ordinary man. Every morning he came up with something new.

Boris was lying face down on the sofa, with one hand on the big sheet of cardboard covering the aquarium, which he had placed right next to him on the coffee table. The two cats, who'd grudgingly given up their usual spot, were sitting on the coffee table, their noses up against the glass. Tails twitching, they watched attentively as the fish twisted and turned. Their obvious intention, if Boris let his vigilance slip for so much as a nanosecond, was to revise his entire mathematical theory, to simplify his calculations by two units. Only Brutus, as loyal as can be, lay purring on Boris's back.

Julie went into the kitchen on tiptoes. She switched on her little radio. Not loudly, just enough to find out if, by some miracle, this might all continue.

'Contrary to all expectations, the ice storm that has been raging for the last two days seems to be lessening in intensity. Hundreds of Hydro-Québec team workers are hard at it, restoring power to as many households as possible. They estimate they will be able to reconnect close to three hundred thousand today.'

She just muttered, through clenched teeth, 'Isn't that typical Hydro-Québec? When you call them, they take forever to come, and when you don't call them, they come before they ought to.'

Julie sincerely hoped that every apartment in Quebec would soon have comfort and electricity . . . with one exception.

You don't quit a job where you're making five hundred dollars a night only to find yourself, the next morning, living with the fear that someone is going to leave.

Just then, Boris walked into the kitchen.

'Morning!'

'Morning.'

'Is something wrong?'

'No, no, everything's fine . . .'

'No, there's something wrong, I can tell!'

When his fish were swimming happily around the tank, Boris's life went swimmingly, too. There had been something handsome about him when he'd been sad and afraid. And now that he was joyful, he was even more handsome. Yesterday he had told her about how he first came to Quebec, his short career in the junior hockey league. She thought it was terrible that he'd been let go after his first inter-team match, after scoring four goals, three of which were during short-handed play. But Julie knew that Boris must be lying about his talent. She'd seen dozens of hockey players at Sex Paradisio, and they always came in threes. Apparently it relaxed them, after a match, to go to a strip club, especially when they were in the NHL. She saw right away that Boris had neither the build nor the eagle eye of a great champion.

'I thought of something, this morning . . .'

'Yes, Boris.'

'Here, you have power, which is great. But it could stop at any time . . .'

'Anything can stop at any time, you're so right, Boris . . .'

'Hold my arm, please.'

Some people view male chivalry as nothing more than a condescending attitude towards the weaker sex. Julie liked chivalry not only because she was fed up with slaps on the bum but above all because there was a lot of ice and it really was slippery. From the moment they left the house, she did not let go of her knight's arm. What astonished her was the way other men were looking at them: in their eyes it was no longer, 'God, I'd like to do her!' that she saw, but, 'What a lucky guy!'

As they walked, she thought again about the night before and the lovely, ordinary little meal they'd had, like a real couple. She'd cooked, he'd done the washing up, and they'd talked about other things besides ice hockey.

'I left Russia because I had no future there. Under communism, researchers were the elite of the country. They were offered big apartments, good salaries, good working conditions. But after the collapse of the Soviet Union all those privileges disappeared. I shouldn't tell you this, and you keep it to yourself, but not everything was so bad under communism . . .'

Julie had promised she wouldn't tell a soul. But she didn't tell him that as far as she was concerned, the fall of the Berlin Wall and the collapse of the Soviet empire suited her fine. For one thing, she was very happy that millions of people would now know what it was like to live in a democracy.

119

But the most important thing was that, thanks to Gorbachev and his perestroika, Boris had been able to leave the country and move in across the street.

Then Boris told her about the rationing that had been their daily bread until 1990, how you could only buy goods from the state shops, where poverty was rife.

'It was awful, inhumane—just like Canada Dépôt!'

Seeing Boris so sad, as he recalled all the worst things about daily life under communism, Julie decided to suggest to her Russian a little trip together, to the very place where he had thrown in the towel earlier.

*   *   *

Clinging to Boris's arm like a mussel to its rock, Julie knew just what to do. She was better than anyone at defending an individual's rights, since she herself had so often suffered from a total disregard for her own rights.

'Can you show me where it says that I can only buy two gas canisters?'

'It doesn't say so anywhere, Miss! It's an order from the manager.'

'I want to speak to the manager!'

'There's no point, he'll only tell you the same thing.'

'I want to speak to the manager!'

'You have to take others into consideration . . .'

'Well, we'll see about that!'

While Boris looked on, stunned, Julie began to empty the shelf of gas canisters. She left the floor manager no option: he grabbed his walkie-talkie and now the entire store knew what was going on.

'I've got an emergency over in Camping Goods! Will the manager please come to Camping Goods!'

Boris, worried, rubbed the back of his neck and turned to Julie, who was still filling the shopping trolley.

'Ten canisters should get us through the night . . .'

'Don't you start, you're not in Russia any more!'

'Now what?'

Boris turned and found himself face to face with the manager, who was looking around, disappointed not to have more of an audience. In fact, there was no audience at all.

'You again! I thought I explained how things work here! So, you take two gas canisters, you go to the till, don't forget your Canada Dépôt tokens, and you don't come back until tomorrow!'

Julie chose that moment to turn around.

'Are you the store manager?'

'Bambi!'

Now the manager was looking left and right, relieved he didn't have more of an audience. For a moment Julie stared at the gas bottles, then took one and jiggled it in her palm.

'Tell me, Freddy, does your wife work here too?'

Freddy understood right away. You can be store manager at Canada Dépôt and like pretty girls. That's not a crime; at worst, it might be a sin. But if the wife finds out, it's not a crime, it's far worse than that.

'So how are your fish doing?'

The cashier immediately recognised Boris and greeted him with a big smile and a wink. Julie did not appreciate such aquariophilic familiarity.

121

The manager's gaze was darting around the shop, terrified. Was he afraid his wife might show up, or was it that a customer might notice he was allowing a massive sale that completely contradicted his grand speech about Quebecker solidarity? Boris was like a kid, watching admiringly as the gas canisters piled up in his shopping bags. The cashier was jubilant.

'Two plus two, plus two, plus two, plus two . . .'

'That's enough now, we get the point!'

In a moment of utter defeat, a manager rarely has any manners, so he picks on those who are weaker than he is.

'Hurry up now! Good jobs are hard to come by these days!'

The cashier said no more, looked down, and finished totalling up in silence. But then she spoke, loud and clear.

'That's twenty-eight canisters at a dollar ninety-nine for a total of sixty-four dollars and nine cents. Cash or credit?'

'Maybe you could give us a discount for buying in bulk?'

'You'd do better to hold your horses, you Russian!'

'Freddy! His name is Boris and I'd like you to give him a nice discount.'

The manager went up close to Julie. He really did not want anyone to overhear.

'Okay, Bambi, you calm down right now.'

'Actually, you never answered my question, about whether your wife works here?'

'I would never have thought you could do something like this.'

'Freddy, I'll let you in on a secret . . . Neither did

122

I!'

The manager stepped back, surprised. He turned to the cashier.

'Ten per cent!'

'I meant a big discount, honey!'

'Twenty . . .'

The cashier, typing away, began to whistle as if everything were perfectly normal.

'Fifty-one dollars and twenty-seven cents!'

Boris paid, beaming. The manager, on seeing the notes, moved closer to Julie again with a greedy expression on his face.

'Well, I want my little discount tonight, too . . .'

'Too late, I quit.'

'Huh?'

Until this moment, the ice storm had been a gift of fate. The best sales ever in two days, better even than Boxing Day. And the little cherry on the cake was that he could lie to his wife with impunity, using the pretext of long nights stocking shelves in order to go and relax at Sex Paradisio. Freddy turned to look at his staff. He saw the first cashier whispering to the next cashier, who in turn went to whisper into the ear of yet another cashier. Intermittently they all turned to look at him. He put on his loud manager's voice.

'Are you going to go on staring at me like that until the spring sales? Go and serve your customers!'

In the end, a store manager's true nature always prevails. After glaring defiantly at his staff of cashiers, some of whom could not stop laughing, Freddy walked past the empty shelves where the gas canisters used to be. Satisfied, he rubbed his hands. The freezing rain had stopped falling this

123

morning. He had a gigantic stock of gas canisters to sell. Twenty-eight in one go, that really helps to empty out the stock room. And this evening at Sex Paradisio he'd find someone to replace Bambi soon enough. Come to think of it, Cassandra had big tits, too.

*   *   *

Business is business.

I WAS NO ONE NOW

'Must be a really cool sofa!'

I should never have told Alex about my mum's spreadsheet. Normally he never said anything about other people's private lives. That's what I liked about him. The only reason I'd told him was because I didn't expect him to say anything.

'How else did you expect them to go about it?'

His matter-of-fact tone hurt.

'When you split up, you have to share what you have, right?'

Maybe I hadn't made myself clear that I felt like I was being compared to a sofa. My first thought was to get revenge. I looked at Alex, but the truth is that he hits too hard, so I only said it in my head:

Your mum left with nothing, and your dad's been left with not much at all. And the not much at all— that's you!

He saw I was giving him a nasty look, but he smiled as if he could see why I was angry. He was like some priest in a movie. I looked out at the street. The little tree was now bent double with the weight of the ice. Its top was touching the ground. Like me, it had no way to defend itself. In the end I'd been right to ask the sky to stop. Poor little tree . . . Would it right itself, or would it stay broken in two for the rest of its life? It was too sad; we had to talk about something else.

'How are things going with the two brothers?'

'Well your dad got it wrong, that's for sure . . .'

My dad couldn't even get something as simple as gossiping about the neighbours right.

'They're a homosexual couple.'

'Queers?'

He looked at me the way only a professor of ethics could.

'A homosexual couple, I said!'

'Same thing.'

'No, it's not the same thing . . .'

'Since when is it not the same thing?'

'Since my dad told me so.'

He smiled, happy. He was proud to be able to tell me that his dad had finally taught him something.

'He really likes Simon. I think it was something he needed, like, to have a friend. You can tell him everything . . .'

He looked at me, as if to apologise.

'But in return, he can tell you everything, too . . .'

I realised he was talking about the sofa again.

'This morning my dad had completely changed. He woke up in a good mood.' Alex looked serene. 'So that put me in a good mood.'

He gave me such a sweet look; I didn't know he could be like that. He raised his eyes heavenwards, as if to thank the sky. Then suddenly he was just like a kid again.

'Why has the ice stopped falling?'

'I don't know.'

Alex was sure I was lying. He had seen me at work with the educational director.

'Have you lost your magical powers?'

'It wasn't magical powers.'

'So why has the ice stopped falling?'

A Hydro-Québec truck pulled out of the side street. Inside were three men who looked pleased with a job well done. Too pleased for Alex . . .

'What have you done!'

He turned around all of a sudden. The light in the stairway of his duplex was on. The power had been restored to his building.

'Why'd you do that?'

'I didn't do anything—'

'I know it was you!'

In just a few seconds he'd gone back to being the old Alex. He always had that tone of voice when he was about to strike. I looked away, defeated.

'I asked it to stop.'

'But why?'

'It wasn't doing anything for me.'

'Did you ever wonder whether maybe it was doing something for other people?'

I could have reminded him about all those people who'd lost power. But the truth was, I'd asked for the ice storm for my sake alone. Now Alex, twisting my collar in his fist, was doing the same thing—thinking only about himself.

'You'd better make that effing ice start falling again. Got it, shortarse?'

He gave me a shove, then got up and opened the door that led to the stairs to his house. He switched off the light. He looked at me to make sure I'd got the message. In his eyes I could read the list of all the risks I was taking. He went across the street and knocked on the door where the homosexual couple lived.

'Come on in, Alex my boy! Finished your little walk already?'

'Yes!'

'Look how happy Pipo is to see you!'

Alex went in. The door closed behind him. Why was the ice storm changing other people's lives and not mine?

127

I didn't even have time to think before the door opened again. I was hoping it was him coming to say sorry, but Pipo bounded out of the door. Alex, with the lead in his hand, gave me a really mean look, then he watched as Pipo had a long wee.

'Pipo, sit!'

Once he'd finished, Pipo did as he was told. Alex twirled his hand above the little dog.

'Roll over!'

Pipo began rolling over on the ice. Alex snapped his fingers and looked at me with his cruel little smile.

'Crawl!'

Pipo was the one who obeyed, but I knew that Alex was really talking to me. I had only one real friend in life, and I didn't want to lose him. I stared at Alex and then I raised my eyes to the sky. I looked at it for a long time. Then I shouted, to be sure Alex could hear me.

'Abracadabra! The sky will win!'

It just came to me like that. I didn't want Alex to think I wasn't doing things properly. He gave a smug little smile, then he leaned over to Pipo, who was still crawling like crazy.

'Good dog, good dog.'

I looked at Alex. I was waiting for my reward, but he just lowered his gaze. He wasn't proud.

No one was proud of hurting me, but they all did it anyway. I didn't give a damn what the sky did now. It had never done anything for me. On the contrary, it had destroyed me. I was worth the same as a stupid sofa, and my only friend was treating me like a dog.

*   *   *

I was no one now.

NO ONE CAN UNDERSTAND
EVERYTHING

After he'd cleaned out Canada Dépôt's supply of gas canisters, Boris insisted on inviting Julie to lunch in a little Russian restaurant, to thank her for her valuable help.

'I don't know what you said to that manager, but you sure know how to talk to men!'

'Not all men, Boris . . .'

It was the sort of place you could find only in Montreal, a little corner of authentic Russia thousands of miles from the Volga. Here, if you were Russian, you could drink vodka the way you did there. The cooking was just like the cooking there. And, just like in Russia, there was a thriving black market. While a Russian might manage to get out of Russia, Russia never got out of a Russian. They couldn't help it: whatever they could buy on the black market was bound to be better than anything you bought at a state-run store. As a sort of gesture of respect for the motherland, no self-respecting Russian immigrant shopped at Canada Dépôt. At this little bar you could buy candles, batteries, generators . . . but no gas canisters.

If Boris had known this, he would have invited Julie to Belle Province for poutine.

With a trained eye, Igor, the proprietor, watched the couple come in, their arms laden with plastic carrier bags full of gas canisters. He led them quickly into the kitchen. At the stove the chef—canary blond with raven-black roots—looked up and then went back to cutting slices of a splendid carp with

130

her huge knife. Julie caught a whiff of the onions in paprika that were sizzling in a huge stewpot.

'What's this yummy thing you're making?'

'Breaded carp onions!'

'I'm not wild about onions, what else do you have?'

'Breaded carp onions!'

You don't argue with a Russian chef, especially when she's giving you a dirty look. Julie turned back to Igor and Boris. Even without understanding the language, she could tell that Russian brotherhood had just been sacrificed upon the altar of greed. From their tone and their gestures, Julie understood everything. Igor wanted to buy the gas canisters. He was holding out two twenty-dollar bills to Boris.

'*Daï!*'

'*Nyet!*'

'*Nyet???*'

With a rueful smile, Igor pulled out a ten-dollar bill and added it to the two twenties. From Boris's gestures and the passion flashing in his eyes, Julie could tell he was expounding on his topological theory. Igor grabbed Boris by the neck.

'You want your four fish to join Olga's carp in the stewpot?'

Olga gripped the knife handle harder and stared calmly at Julie. It was the sort of calm that makes it abundantly clear that a shift from word to deed would be a mere formality.

Boris, clearly shaken, had no choice but to relent. Once Igor had summarily relieved Boris of his carrier bags, reducing his stock to only two canisters, just as if he were back at Canada Dépôt, Olga stepped in to show who was in charge in that

131

kitchen.

'You're not going to let his fish die!'

Sheepishly, Igor handed Boris a bag with eight canisters, and Boris handed back the ten-dollar bill. Women really had a thing about Boris's mathematical theory. Olga took two plates and heaped them high.

Boris and Julie sat at a quiet table off to one side and sampled Olga's carp, on the house. The onions, prepared by this chef who'd come from the cold, were not as strong as Julie had feared. One thing was for sure: with Boris everything tasted good, and she was never bored. Between two fish bones, she took the plunge.

'Have you got a girlfriend?'

'Not that I know of . . .'

She wanted to shout, Open your eyes, Boris, you know who she is, she's sitting right here opposite you!

But with her mouth full of carp, that would be a perilous venture. Besides, she didn't feel like shouting while her breath smelled of onions. So she savoured her food, and took her time. Love is like a taxi: if it doesn't stop when you run after it, then it's already taken. To catch one you just have to wait in the right spot.

*   *   *

'The power is back on in your place . . .'

'I must have left the light on when the power went out.'

Boris looked through the window into the lit room. He pursed his lips and turned to Julie.

'I don't want to inconvenience you any longer,'

he said formally.

'You're no inconvenience.'

'I know.'

Boris Bogdanov was not a macho man, he was merely pragmatic. She understood this, and his reply didn't surprise her. When you want to love, you must know how to do it, but to know how, you have to ask. So Julie threw a fastball straight at the heart of this logical man, this man who seemed to be made of marble.

'My flat is on the same grid as the old people's home, but yours isn't. You may have power at your place now, but there's no telling when it might go out again. Maybe we should wait a little before repatriating your fish?'

Boris didn't quite understand. The equation still contained too many unknowns. Julie's only chance was to try an inside curveball.

'The likelihood . . . uh . . . let's say the *probability* that the power will go out is far greater for your place than for mine.'

Boris immediately rubbed his forehead then started pacing in a circle. He was doing complicated calculations in his head, muttering quotients and square roots in Russian. Then suddenly he fell silent, but not for long.

'*Da . . . Da . . . Da . . .*'

'I can always ask Michel, my neighbour—he works for the weather office.'

'Do you have something to drink that will warm me up?'

'I have everything you need to warm you up . . .'

Boris Bogdanov didn't get it, not at all.

'*Davai!*'

133

*   *   *

No one can understand everything.

I DIDN'T WANT TO WAIT

'Tonight's forecast has dealt us a nasty surprise: we're in for more freezing rain.'

The sky had heard me. I'd done it, I really had done it! Now there could be no doubt about it.

'We can expect the worst; experts over at Météo Canada are forecasting at least ten millimetres of freezing rain for Montreal and the entire region.'

What on earth was the sky up to now? I had just asked it to give Alex a hand, but it didn't have to go so far! Some ice on the building across the street—that would have been more than enough.

'Emergency shelters are expecting thousands of people tonight. Let's go straight to our report on . . .'

It gave me a shock to see all those people lying on camp beds, or lining up to go to the showers. It was like pictures from somewhere else, anywhere but Quebec. Normally, human misery is far away. Then I saw this little kid who was crying because he'd lost his parents at the shelter.

And I started crying with him.

When they said the little kid had found his mummy and daddy that didn't stop my tears. The thought that I'd caused this pain to others just caused me even more pain. Especially as I had done what I'd done just so I'd *stop* feeling pain. I should have stood up to Alex, I should have said no. I choked on my tears.

Then I felt an arm around me. I opened my eyes. Through my tears I saw my mum. She looked desperate, terrified to see me crying. Apparently, when a child is hurting, his mother starts hurting

135

just the same.

'What's the matter, sweetie?'

'It's all my fault!'

'No it isn't, it's not your fault!'

'It's all because of me!'

'You had nothing to do with it.'

'I did, I did, I know I did . . .'

'You mustn't feel guilty, sweetheart . . .'

'You don't understand—'

My mum put her hands on my cheeks and squeezed. I couldn't finish my sentence. In her eyes there were tears, just about to spill.

'Darling, let me tell you again, don't blame yourself, you had nothing to do with it.'

'I'll never forgive myself.'

I dried my tears. I took a deep breath. I had to get it off my chest, this terrible thing I'd done.

'Mum, I'm the one who—'

'Stop saying that, you'll make me cry!'

Too late: she was already crying. It was the first time I'd ever really seen her cry. In fact, grown-ups cry just the same as kids. I felt awful, it was all my fault.

'Mum, please forgive me for what I did—'

She had trouble speaking through her tears.

'But I told you, you haven't done anything wrong! So stop saying that!'

With her hands on my cheeks, she gave me a little shake. She really wanted me to agree with her.

'That's the truth! None of it is your fault, not any of it!'

I pulled free of her hands and looked at the television.

'*Hospital emergency services are overwhelmed with victims of the black ice, and are treating a constant*

136

succession of sprains, fractures and head injuries. One man is in a deep coma at Sacré-Coeur Hospital after he fell while trying to de-ice the roof of his summer cottage in the Laurentides.'

I didn't have to look at my mum for very long to see that she and I were both thinking the same thing.

'Did you talk to him today?'

'No, he didn't call . . .'

Suddenly I was really frightened. There are worse things than parents splitting up, and one of them is having no parents at all. My mum closed her eyes. I'm sure she was praying. I don't believe in God, but I prayed, too.

Knock-knock!

We turned to the door. We heard the knock all right.

'Police! Open up!'

My mum leaped up and looked at me. My dad had often told us the protocol. When it's an injury, even a serious one, the police call you on the phone. When they knock on your door, it's to tell you the worst.

'Stay there, honey.'

She ran to the door, took a deep breath, or maybe I should say gathered her courage. She opened the door. Then she took a step back, and cried out.

'Oh no!'

The sky fell on my head. I saw all the rest in slow motion. My dad walked in, like a soldier returning from the war, both his arms in a cast and a sling.

'Do you have any idea what a fright you gave us?'

'It was to make sure you'd open up.'

Police humour is a male thing. My mum didn't

laugh.

'I hope you don't think we've reached that point.'

My dad was a mess, but I was so relieved. He'd come back. My parents stared at each other for a long time. This was one situation they hadn't predicted either. Finally Dad turned to me.

'Are you going to wait until these casts come off to give me a kiss?'

*   *   *

I didn't want to wait.

HE WAS ABOUT TO FIND OUT

'Yoo-hoo! I'm in here!'

'Alexis, just give me time to take off my coat and hat and mittens.'

Simon smiled: his evacuee still needed to talk. He found Michel in the kitchen and went over to give him a gentle slap on the bum.

'What's this lovely meal you're preparing?'

'*Escalopes Volpini* with white wine.'

'The best in town!'

'No, the best is . . .' Michel turned to face Simon, who held up his mouth, tenderly, '. . . the little evening kiss!'

While Michel was turning the escalopes, Simon stroked his shoulder, and they stayed like that for a moment, close, happy, relieved.

The evening before, when Simon had joined Michel in bed, he had given him the gist of his conversation with Alexis. A psychoanalyst is not supposed to do this, but since his client was unaware of what was actually going on, Simon was practising in secret and was therefore not bound by the pledge of confidentiality.

'Did you tell him we're gay?'

'You think he didn't notice?'

'Then the whole neighbourhood will find out.'

'So?'

'And what if the association finds out?'

'So, let the association find out. This ice storm is giving us a chance to come out of hiding.'

Michel could not help but wipe away a tear. He had always been the more sensitive of the two. He had been waiting for this moment for so long that he'd stopped believing it would ever come. It is a noble thing to want others to accept you, but first you must accept yourself.

'Is that why you offered to take them in?'

'Of course not. I just wanted to help out . . .'

Michel knew his Simon by heart, and in his heart he knew he was far too intelligent not to have thought the whole thing through when he first offered to help his neighbours. Welcoming Alex and Alexis to their home would be their way of coming out to the neighbourhood.

What Simon couldn't have foreseen, however, was how completely dependent Alexis would become on their improvised sessions of psychoanalysis.

*   *   *

'Yoo-hoo! The bottle is waiting!'

'I'm coming, Alexis, I'm coming!'

On his way to the couch in the study, Simon caught sight of Alex playing with Pipo.

'Michel said there's gonna be tons more freezing rain tonight!'

'Tons?'

'We've got power back in our house but my dad says it'll go out again before long.'

'If your dad says so . . .'

'Michel says it's okay if we stay. And he works at Météo Canada. So he knows what he's talking about.'

'You're right. When it comes to the forecast, caution is the best counsellor.'

Even a psychoanalyst can make others believe he

is helping them when actually he is helping himself. He'll hide his true motivations, unremorsefully.

'I think Pipo would be really sad if you left us.'

In the sitting room, Simon went over to the stereo. After rifling through the huge collection of records, he chose *Carmen*. From among the dozen or so different versions he had of Bizet's opera, he chose the performance by Maria Callas from 1964. It was a historic recording of an opera the diva had never sung in public, and here she sang it with a voice that would make you weep. Then he abruptly changed his mind: perhaps this wasn't the right time to play such an emotional piece around such a sensitive patient.

'Did you know I made a record, Simon?'

'No, I didn't know that.'

'Nobody knows . . .'

'Tell me about it, Alexis.'

Alexis slumped deeper into the couch and stretched out his legs.

'May I?'

'Sure, go ahead.'

Alexis placed his feet gently on the coffee table, careful not to disturb anything. He closed his eyes, the better to think back to his *yéyé* years of French pop in the 1960s.

Rrrring!

'Shit!'

'Don't worry, Alexis, Michel will get the door. Just relax . . .'

Annoyed, Alexis could not keep from tapping his fingers on the armrest. Simon took the precious bottle of Chivas Royal Salute 21 Year Old from its box. With a grimace he filled Alexis's glass. After a few minutes, Michel came in.

141

'It was the young lady from next door, asking me for my forecast for the night.'

'I bet you told her there's going to be tons of freezing rain.'

'You lose. I only said kilos. But I got the impression it made her happy she'd be able to hang on to her Russian tenant.'

'I hope he didn't have time to go and buy any booze, otherwise we won't get any sleep.'

'Speaking of booze . . .'

Simon handed Michel the empty whisky bottle. Alexis chose that moment to empty his glass in one go. At a hundred and fifty-nine dollars a bottle, Michel was right to grimace. But you can't put a price on a coming-out party, even just a neighbourhood one.

'It's there to be drunk!'

Simon waited for Michel to return to his *escalopes Volpini,* and in lieu of an aperitif he turned back to his patient on the couch.

'So you were saying you made a record?'

Alexis decided to answer by singing.

'Ils disent qu'on était jeunes et qu'on ne savait pas . . . Ne nous découvrons pas jusqu'à ce qu'on grandisse—'

Sobs momentarily interrupted the performance. Simon hastily applauded.

'That's really great!'

'That's not all! There's a chorus, it's coming.'

'Oh?'

'Bébé! . . . Je t'ai, toi, bébé . . . Je t'ai, toi, bébé . . .'

Alex jumped. That was his song. About his mother and him!

'Je t'ai, toi, pour me prendre la main . . .
Je t'ai, toi, pour comprendre . . .

142

Je t'ai, toi, pour marcher avec moi . . .
Je t'ai, toi, pour me serrer fort . . .'
The second time the chorus came round was harder going: Alexis's sobs made his words incomprehensible. Maybe it was just as well.

'*Bé . . . Je . . . bé . . . t'ai . . . bé . . . toi . . . bé . . .'*
Alex blocked his ears. He didn't want to hear any more. He wasn't the only one.

'Alexis, I think we can stop there. It's making Pipo cry.'

When silence fell, the sound of giggling came clearly from the kitchen; those must have been the funniest *escalopes Volpini* ever made. But Simon wanted to avoid hurting Alexis's feelings at all costs. Providential patients like this one must be nurtured.

'It's a beautiful song. Did you write it?'

'You didn't recognise it?'

'No . . . Should I have?'

'It's the French version of "I Got You Babe" by Sonny and Cher.'

'That's odd, I don't remember it sounding like that.'

'Because this is the disco version!'

From the study, where Pipo had sprawled out on his lap, Alex heard his dad telling his life story in a way he'd never told it before. And so he found out that his mother and father had made a record together.

'How did it do?'

'Complete fiasco, we didn't even sell a hundred copies. My basement is full of them.'

'And how did you deal with the lack of success, Alexis?'

'I didn't deal, it was an *or*deal, more like.'

'You have to learn from failure. It can be an opportunity to help you build your future.'

'Well, in my case it destroyed it.'

'Tell me about it, Alexis.'

There was no more laughter coming from the kitchen. Michel had decided that for once he would not serve the *escalopes Volpini* medium rare. A true confession is like Greek tragedy: it's a rare, intense moment that lasts only a certain length of time. And if you miss it, you won't ever capture it again.

'She was nineteen, full of life, so beautiful. She'd worked really hard to come here from Mexico to study. She was a painter. She hadn't even been here a month. I was singing in a bar. She walked in, she was so pure, I didn't want to sing for anyone but her . . .'

Alex left the study, Pipo following behind. He went into the sitting room and sat down next to his father, not saying a thing. Simon held his breath, observing Alexis's reaction. Michel poked his head around the door from the kitchen. Even Pipo realised the significance of the moment when a person's hidden side becomes illuminated, and he stretched out on the floor. Simon lowered his voice to a whisper.

'Go on, Alexis . . .'

*   *   *

Alex's heart began to pound. He was about to find out.

CAN YOU FIX IT FOR ME?

'Do you know why cats always land on their paws?'

'No, Dad.'

'Because they know how!'

Two days in the cold weather had transformed my dad. I didn't recognise him. He was even managing to poke fun at himself. That must be one of the virtues of being deep-frozen. Once you thaw out, there's nothing left but joy. He couldn't stop waving his wrists around in their casts. He looked like a puppet, but he was real and there were no strings attached any more.

'Want to play Monopoly?'

When was the last time I played Monopoly with my dad?

'Come on, come and play with us!'

When was the last time I'd played Monopoly with both of them? Probably never. In my mother's opinion it wasn't educational enough.

'It's just capitalism dressed up as a game! Wouldn't Trivial Pursuit be better?'

'With my hands in casts Trivial Pursuit isn't very practical.'

I could tell my mum was wondering if it was really my dad sitting across from her.

'Yes, Dad's right, I'd rather play Monopoly. All three of us.'

I put on my whiny little voice, the one from back when I used to try and charm my mum in order to get my way. Dad gestured towards me with his casts as if I were the bearer of some universal truth. My mum sat down. She'd surrendered. But she still had to have the last word.

'All right, but not for long!'

I sped to my bedroom for the box, brought it back, opened it and set out the banknotes on the coffee table in the sitting room. My dad took the top hat as his token and left me the car. He handed my mum the thimble.

'Off to a good start . . .'

'Who'll put the dice on my cast?'

'I have to sort my money, Dad!'

He held his palms in their casts out to my mum.

'Which one do you want to play with?'

'The white one!'

She looked up at the sky—the ceiling, rather— then put both dice on my dad's right cast. I saw the way my mum looked at him when he tossed the dice. Then suddenly we heard an animal-roar.

'Double six!'

My dad landed on Chance. I took the card from the pile and, not looking at it, set it down in front of him.

'You take top prize in a beauty contest, collect one thousand dollars from each player!'

I took a thousand from my pile of money and placed it on my dad's pile. My mum picked up the dice. My dad gave her a gentle shove with his cast.

'You owe a thousand dollars to the best-looking guy in the gang.'

'Here! Take your thousand bucks. Bad debts make bad friends. We need to talk about that, actually . . .'

I couldn't help but look at the sofa. Still pleased with her answer, my mum cupped her hands around the dice. My dad acted as if he hadn't heard.

'It's still my turn, I threw double. The dice!'

My mum handed him the dice without a word. I know what she was thinking: Monopoly is a barbaric game that fosters nothing but greed and stupidity.

'Double six!'

'Could you try not to burst my eardrums every time you throw the dice?'

'Sorry, darling!'

My father was the only one who didn't hear what he'd just said. My mum watched the white plaster pushing the top hat onto Community Chest. I didn't wait for Dad to ask, and I put the card from the top of the pile in front of him. My mum looked at me, she knew I'd heard, but above all she'd noticed that I could tell it had annoyed her.

'This is your lucky day, receive a thousand dollars from every player!'

Maybe my dad got a little too big for his breeches after that.

'Luck smiles on those who know how to make the most of it! Roll the dice!'

He shut up when he had to go straight to jail without passing Go. Three doubles in Monopoly is fatal. He looked a bit sheepish, to my mum's great satisfaction.

'You'll see, you'll like it there.'

He started whistling, to make light of it all.

'It's definitely nicer here than at the cottage!'

My feelings exactly.

*   *   *

As for my mum, those were anything but her feelings when my dad asked her to help him get washed.

147

'I can't wash with my casts! I'll ruin them!'

'Just be careful.'

'I haven't been able to take a shower in two days, I can't go on like this!'

I could hear them while I was putting the money away in the box. My mum had won. Even at Monopoly, it's the thinkers who end up winning.

'No way. I will not help you wash!'

I heard my mum opening a cupboard in the kitchen. Then she came back into the sitting room.

'Have you got any tape in your school things?'

She wrapped my dad's hands in two plastic bags from Canada Dépôt. She was careful to make sure everything was hermetically sealed. My dad followed her all the way to the bathroom. She turned on the water in the shower.

'And how am I supposed to take my shirt off with these Canada Dépôt mittens?'

You can be smart and still not think of everything. She didn't get angry; she could see it was funny. But just because something is funny doesn't mean it will change your mind.

'Let your son help you!'

Slam! She left the two of us together. My dad leaned forward and I started pulling off his shirt. We struggled to get it past the casts. His T-shirt was a little easier.

'I'm glad you're here, Dad.'

'Me too. I'm glad to see you again.'

He reached for his belt. Even with his fingers in plastic he could still manage to do a few little things.

'I'll manage.'

'If you need me, just shout.'

'I'll shout. Otherwise, what's the point in having

a son?'

*   *   *

One good thing about having a son is that he'll hold the hairdryer over your wet cast. Since my dad couldn't manage with the face flannel, he took a towel to wash himself. After a while the tape came off but he didn't notice that his cast under the wet towel wasn't protected any more.

'It's not burning?'

'No, far from it, it feels gentle and warm.'

I was glad to be taking care of him. He kept looking around, sometimes at me, sometimes over towards the kitchen. Then all around the sitting room, but his eyes no longer came to rest on the television. He hadn't even switched it on.

'Pasta's ready!'

At the table, it didn't take long for my dad to convince us that he couldn't hold his cutlery.

'I already undressed him and dried his cast!'

So my mum held his spoon, and from that point on we didn't say much. The minute he finished one spoonful my dad opened his mouth wide, while my mum slurped hers down in between mouthfuls for my dad. I kept looking at them as if everything were perfectly normal, but in fact it wasn't. My mum was feeding my dad as if he were a little kid, but really I was the little kid, and eating all by myself. After a little while they got into a certain rhythm, and everything seemed to be running smoothly. They didn't need to speak any more, they understood each other. But all good things must come to an end. And here the end came between two mouthfuls.

149

'You should film your mum and dad with your video camera.'

'Martin! I don't think that's a very good idea.'

'You don't think this would make a funny video?'

'Precisely. That's why I don't want to be filmed.'

She put an end to the discussion by shoving the spoon in my dad's mouth and they went on with their little game until his plate was empty. Then my mum got up.

'You've got to start physiotherapy first thing tomorrow or find some other solution, because I have no intention of doing this every day.'

My dad still had his mouth open, then he closed it, then he opened it again. He did a good impression of a goldfish for a few seconds. My mum was already in the sitting room.

'It's bath time!'

I picked up the spoon, but my dad gestured to me to go ahead. I turned the tap on in the bath and let the water run while I went to the sink and wet my hair. I didn't want it to last too long. So it didn't. When I went back out, I knew from the clacking of the keyboard that my mum was back on the computer. Naturally, as soon as she saw me she closed the accounts file.

'Did you have a good scrub all over, darling?'

'Yes, Mum.'

'Go and put on your pyjamas.'

'Yes, Mum.'

'After that go and tell your father to come and help me light the fire.'

'With his casts he won't be able to.'

'He can just tell me what to do.'

I went past my room but I didn't go in, I just continued on to the kitchen. I heard a faint clatter,

150

and went slowly closer. Not only had my dad managed to pick up a fork, he'd also found a way to hold a knife in the other hand. He had taken a piece of cheese from the fridge and was chewing on it greedily while he sliced himself some bread. I stepped back so he wouldn't see me.

'Dad! Mum needs you to light the fire!'

He shoved the cutlery out of sight. *Gling! Glang!* He must have had loads of cheese still in his mouth, and definitely some bread, because he had a hard time talking.

'In the state . . . I'm in . . . I'll do . . . what I can . . . And my cast . . . isn't dry . . . yet.'

It's not just kids who lie when they want to be looked after.

When I left the sitting room, wishing them good night, my dad was sitting next to the fireplace. He was holding his casts above the hearth. My mum was sitting on the sofa, not far away, let's say just behind him.

'What on earth possessed you to do such a foolish thing?'

'I was alone with the ice. After a while you're fed up to here with it!'

'So you decided to de-ice the roof . . .'

They looked at each other and smiled, a smile of complicity for once. The light from the flames was glowing on their faces. They were so beautiful. It was like at the cinema. I always closed my eyes when two adults kissed in a film, because it was embarrassing. But this time I wouldn't close my eyes if they kissed. I waited. I wanted them to kiss for a long time, with the words 'The End' floating above them in big white letters. I was sorry I didn't have my video camera.

151

But life isn't like the movies. My mum switched on the light.

'I'll get you everything you need for the sofa, but I warn you, I will not help you change channels on that television every three seconds!'

It would have been nicer to film a kiss.

'Why do you want me to watch television?'

'I don't know . . . You always do, don't you?'

'Thanks, but I'll manage.'

For the first time, I understood what the sky was trying to tell me. The ice storm hadn't been able to stop my dad from leaving the house, but it had fixed things so he would come back. Being frozen had changed him. My mum found it hard to believe. I could see it in her eyes when she brought him a blanket and a pillow.

'It's as if . . . you're not how you used to be.'

'That's quite possible . . .'

'I can understand that you're glad to be here, but don't forget our mutual agreement.'

She handed him a printed piece of paper. It was the spreadsheet. About the sofa, and all that stuff.

'I hope this won't keep you awake.'

In bed I did a lot of thinking. My mum, for a start, hadn't been deep-frozen. And as long as she wasn't deep-frozen she wouldn't change. I got up, and looked out at my friend the sky.

*   *   *

'Can you fix it for me?'

Thursday, 8 January 1998

'The ice storm has renewed its intensity. Every record has been broken. In the region of Montreal, pylons have been collapsing one after the other. A total blackout is feared for the island. The majority of businesses in the centre of town closed down at noon to save electricity. There are concerns about a possible shortage of drinking water. The Canadian Armed Forces have been called to the rescue. At the end of today already a million households, or roughly two and a half million people, are without power.'

SOMETIMES LIFE IS JUST LIKE THE MOVIES

'Watch out!'

Without warning the branch bent beneath the weight of the incessant freezing rain. Boris grabbed hold of Julie with both hands to throw her to the ground, protecting her with his body as the huge branch fell on top of them. *Crash!* Boris was pinned to the ground, and could not pull away from Julie.

'Julie, are you all right?'

'Mmmmm . . .'

Julie's eyes were closed. A blissful smile lit up her lovely face, which was framed by a few stray strands of hair. Pure mathematics research does not include first aid classes, but the state the young woman was in was not unlike the one Boris had been in at Val-d'Or at the time of his pathetic performance in the Quebec Major Junior League.

'Julie, wake up!'

'Mmmmm . . .'

Boris realised the situation was serious. Pressing with his hands, he tried to push the huge branch away. But even for a natural born physicist, wood is just plain heavy, and ice is even heavier. The branch moved only a few inches, and then resumed its previous position. Boris's strength gave out, and he found himself lying against Julie once again. When she opened her eyes, her expression was one of total purity.

'I didn't know that paradise was all white.'

'You're not in paradise—a huge branch has fallen on top of us.'

Julie may have been under a branch, but more than anything she was in shock.

'I never knew it could be so lovely to be stuck under a branch; did you, Boris?'

They had stayed up late into the night watching over the fish, and they'd emptied half a bottle of port and an entire bottle of ouzo that a Greek client had given Julie. She had tried to be open with Boris, to express how lucky she was to have met him. Boris conceded he was also glad to have made her acquaintance. But . . .

'I've been working on my theory for years now, I can't afford to get distracted when I am so near my goal.'

'I understand.'

A few hundred kilos of wood and ice on her head soon made Julie forget what she had claimed to understand.

'It's so nice here under this sky full of ice, don't you think, Boris?'

'That remains to be seen. Perhaps it's not the *best* place . . . and it's starting to get cold . . .'

'Our hearts will keep us warm.'

'Are you sure you're all right, Julie?'

'I've never been better.'

Boris heard other branches creaking. All this creaking and groaning was very stressful. It made you think that the worst could happen at any moment. *Crash!* Another branch fell only a few inches away.

'I love this music, Boris.'

Boris didn't have the heart to joke, or to try to convince Julie that this music might be the opening chords of a mournful requiem in their honour. Like many immigrants, Boris called out in the first

156

language that came to mind—but oddly enough, it wasn't Russian, but English.

'*Help!*'

Julie murmured sweetly, '*I need somebody . . .*'

'*Help!*'

'*Not just anybody . . .*'

'*Help!*'

'*I need someone . . .*'

Julie would have loved to go on, but Boris had put his hand over her mouth. There is a time for singing and another for getting out of deep shit. Boris wasn't sure whether he was in deep shit, but he knew he was in ice up to his neck.

'Is anyone there?'

The branches went on cracking all around them. For Julie, his refrain was nothing more than sixties nostalgia.

'*Won't you please, please help me . . .*'

She increased the volume by a few decibels.

'*Help meeeeee! Please, help meeeee!*'

'Don't worry, Miss, we're coming to help you!'

Boris Bogdanov felt like an idiot. Why hadn't anyone heard *him*? How infuriating—the faintest little peep out of the woman pinned beneath him and along comes a man, just like that. Boris wanted to take things in hand again. Chivalry, even Russian chivalry, has its limits, because for a start it can only be conjugated in the masculine.

'Hurry, quickly!'

'Oh? There are two of you?'

Boris thought he could hear the disappointment in the man's voice. The sort of disappointment a guy feels when he's been watching a woman in a bar for a few minutes and, just when he's about to go up to her, the lovely loner's boyfriend comes out of

157

the loo. Boris was probably not very friendly.

'Something wrong with there being two of us?'

'Just the two of us . . . until the end of time . . .'

'I can't lift the branch, I'll go for help.'

'Hold me close against your body . . .'

To get Julie the diva to stop singing, Boris held her tight. He suddenly felt something inside. Or rather, something coming from him. He observed the lovely girl, deep in her romantic bliss. His mathematical pragmatism could allow only one fundamental question: was she having an effect on him?

While his brain was trying to banish all things illogical—so inimical to the researcher—his feelings became an exponent, the exact value of which he was duty-bound to determine. While supposing that the body he was lying on was as attractive as it was possible to be, he turned for a moment to address the problem in terms of probabilities. What were the odds he would find himself outside his building lying on top of such a beautiful woman, with an ice-covered tree on his back to boot?

But before you can prove that Melanie wees standing up, you must prove that Melanie exists . . .

His uncontrollable erection, to be included in his probability study only with the utmost discretion, confirmed unequivocally that it was a result of Julie's presence beneath him. Therefore, if his erection existed, Julie must exist!

Still lying down, he then approached the problem from a vertical standpoint.

Why was he stuck on top of Julie? Because a tree was holding her there.

Why had the tree crashed down on them? Because there was an ice storm!

Given that no similar meteorological situation had occurred since 1961, given that he had been turned down for thirty-nine apartments before he had found this one, given the number of trees in Montreal, offset by the number of trees shattered by ice over the past three days, take as an index the fact that an ice-covered branch requires three seconds, without warning, to fall off a tree—in other words, it had been one chance in twenty-eight thousand eight hundred that this branch would fall just as they were walking beneath it. Multiplying that by the probability of being pinned beneath a branch big enough to hold down two people, Boris Bogdanov concluded that the probability of feeling this sudden erection because he was lying on top of his neighbour from across the street was only one in thirteen million six hundred and fifty-seven thousand one hundred and fifty-nine. The odds were exactly six thousand six hundred and fifty-seven fewer than getting six numbers out of six in the 6/49 lottery.

Boris shifted his body above Julie to protect her from the little slivers of ice that were falling off the branches. Beneath him lay the possibility, perhaps unique, of no longer living solely for his fish. The branch moved. Then all of a sudden, to a sound of frozen branches unheard since 1961, there came a flash of light.

'Are we disturbing you?'

Before turning to his rescuer, Boris delicately loosened his lovely lady's arms from around his shoulders.

'*Golubchik?*'

Standing above them were Alexis, Simon, Michel and the neighbour from across the way, who had

159

both wrists in plaster.

'Forgive me, but with my wrists like this I couldn't even begin to move the branch. Then when I saw there were two of you I figured it must be really heavy, so I went to get the neighbours from next door . . .'

'It's taken us a while but we couldn't help but hear you singing . . .'

Simon nudged Michel with his shoulder. Boris got to his feet, then helped Julie back up onto her boots. Dreamily, she immediately looped her arms around the neck of her new Slavic love.

'Julie, I'm sorry we interrupted you . . .'

'Really, Michel, it's fine.'

'How on earth did you end up under that branch?'

'We were collecting ice to put in the bath, because we heard that you can't drink the water any more.'

'That's right, the purification plants are down.'

All of a sudden the tension went up a notch, and they looked at each other. The situation was suddenly critical.

'We really are up shit creek.'

'It's as if there's a war on!'

'Think of all the people with kids . . .'

'Or little babies . . .'

'And old people, all alone at home . . .'

'Think of his poor fish!'

That brought the crescendo of miseries due to the lack of drinking water to a sudden halt. Even if the logic required to associate fish with water is pretty basic, no one had thought of it except Julie.

'His fish?'

Julie had regained her composure, and she had

160

plenty to say on the matter. In her ecstatic state she didn't notice that, now and again, like Olga with her carp stuffed with onions, she was using the odd word of Russian. But her Russian scientist's topological theory seemed infinitely abstract to the other men, even when it was being explained by a pretty woman. It was a shock for Boris, suddenly a spectator of his own passion as it was unveiled to everyone around them, a passion in which he had nearly drowned. Holding an ice-encrusted twig, Julie traced the course of each fish, from memory, on the ground. As he listened, Boris watched people walking down the middle of the devastated street, avoiding the falling branches. He heard the infernal menacing, creaking sound, the harbinger of an imminent crash. A procession of soldiers went by in the distance. It reminded him of the darkest hours of the communist regime in Russia. There you did not live—at best you survived.

Where Newton was concerned, Boris felt nothing but the Slavic scorn of a Russian who reproaches the Anglo-Saxons for grabbing all the scientific firsts, but he suddenly decided to view everything as relative.

'Maybe there are more important things in life than my fish?'

Everyone seemed to agree except for Julie. Boris's face became very gentle, illuminated by a new understanding. He smiled at the neighbour who had wanted to help, and whom he'd been ignoring, in spite of the man's injuries.

'What did you do to your wrists, Monsieur?'

*   *   *

161

From the window, Alex could see Martin waving his arms to mime his fall from the roof. Then he went to the stereo and put the arm back in the starting position to play the 45. He wanted to hear Al and Doro again.

*　　　*　　　*

'You could have died in a fall like that!'

'They make us tough in the police.'

'Are you a policeman? With which squadron?'

'The lazybones squadron.'

'There must be a lot of you!'

'Alexis, don't you start! I'm Simon, by the way.'

Simon gingerly looped his hand around the cast held out to him. He was very careful not to shake it.

'And I'm Martin!'

'I'm Julie!'

'I'm Boris!'

'Ouch! Careful with my cast!'

'And I'm Alexis!'

'Yes, I recognise you, you're Alex's dad—he and my son are best friends.'

'Yes, that's right.'

'And I'm Michel.'

'You must be Simon's brother?'

'Not his brother, his boyfriend.'

'You mean his buddy, Alexis.'

Martin wasn't sure he understood. Julie decided to drive the point home.

'His partner, if you prefer.'

All holding their breath, anticipating his reaction, the little group turned to Martin. He did not hesitate for long.

'Very pleased to meet you! It's crazy that it's

162

taken a disaster like this for us to finally get to know each other.'

Michel and Simon shared a look of relief: at last they were rid of the burden of being clandestine. Out in the street, in front of their neighbours, they were holding hands.

*   *   *

Je t'ai bébééééé . . .

This time Alex decided not to listen to the song again. He'd heard it so many times that he could play it in his head. He carefully replaced the record in its sleeve. On the front cover was written *Al and Doro*, in purple against a yellow background. On the photograph, wearing a white shirt with the collar opened wide, Alexis was smiling from one blond sideburn to the other. Next to him, with a white band around her black mane, was Alex's mother, Dorores. Alex traced his mother's lovely face with his finger, then put the record under his pillow. The front door opened.

'Come in, everybody, we're glad you're all here.'

'Are you sure we're not disturbing you?'

'Of course not, there's nothing else to do, anyway. Michel will make us a lovely big dish of spaghetti carbonara!'

'I'll go round to my place and get two bottles and I'll be back.'

'Can you manage with your casts?'

'Yes, don't worry, Alexis.'

Alex went out into the hallway to greet everybody and found them all bumping into each other as they removed their boots. He saw Julie and Boris first, as they had got their shoes off before the

163

others.

'Alex! My little kitten rescuer!'

'You filmed us, too, I hope?'

Alex turned bright red. Boris, still laughing, headed into the sitting room at Simon's invitation. The bubbly Julie waited until the two men had moved away to lean down to Alex.

'So, you were filming me, you naughty boy?'

She ruffled Alex's hair, and, given the circumstances, he had no choice but to let her, even if he didn't like that sort of thing: he was a rebel, after all. Julie rubbed his head harder and harder. Was she about to tell him off and shout at him? Then she tenderly smoothed his tousled hair.

'I hope you'll show me some day, I've always dreamed of being in a film!'

*　　　*　　　*

Sometimes life is just like the movies.

WE QUEBECKERS STICK TOGETHER!

My dad took my mum's arm, under the pretext that he was afraid he'd slip on the ice. Not long before, when I'd looked out of the window at him trying to lift the branch, he seemed to be standing up fine. Just like he'd been fine last night, hiding from us and eating on his own. I liked this little game he was playing. I was glad we were going out the three of us together, even if it had taken Dad some time to convince Mum to come with us.

'You'll see, they're really nice. And besides, what could be more normal than meeting your neighbours?'

'In seven years we've never said a word to them and now we have to go running over there?'

'Exceptional situations make for exceptional encounters.'

'Well, I don't think that girl who lives next door is anything special.'

'She's very nice. She and her boyfriend, that young student from across the street, just had a branch come crashing down on them.'

'Frankly I have no desire to find myself in the same room as Alex's dad. I've said hello to him dozens of times and he never bothers to answer.'

'He's changed a lot, you'll see.'

'Oh, wow, it's an epidemic.'

'Oh, come on, it'll be fun!'

'Damned ice!'

Now my mum stood in front of me holding a bottle of wine in each hand, my dad clutching her shoulder. He stopped her with his arm and

165

whispered something in her ear.

'Well, it looks like we're having one surprise after the other!'

'You'd better tell him, anyway.'

'I think it's better if it's a man who tells him.'

My dad beckoned to me. He didn't want to let go of my mum. He grew suddenly very serious.

'I don't want you to be surprised, but sometimes in life you will come across men who don't always necessarily go out with women. It's their choice. Simon and Michel are . . .'

'A gay couple!'

'You knew?'

'Yes, Alex told me.'

'And what did you think?'

'Nothing! Why should it bother me? They're happy, and *they're* together.'

My mum and dad understood the same thing at the same time. I'd hit the bull's-eye. Neither one wanted to say anything. They were saved by the music.

'Ready to dance?'

Alex's dad came across the street, holding a guitar and, what's more, he had a huge smile on his face. He came up to my parents and held out his hand.

'Hey, Martin! Are you going to introduce me to your wife?'

'Alexis, this is Anne, Anne, may I introduce Alexis.'

'Very pleased to meet you, Anne! Very pleased . . . I haven't always been very friendly. Please forgive me.'

Alexis didn't wait for my mum to reply. He turned quickly to lead the way. Mum looked at Dad, then

166

she spoke to me, as if I was the last one left whom she could confide in.

'What is going on with everybody?'

'What do you mean?'

Alexis, without ringing the bell or even knocking, opened the door to Simon and Michel's place. We heard laughter. Everyone was having a good time. We hurried in. Alexis sat down on the couch with his guitar. After dusting it off, he tuned it quickly, by ear.

'First, a tribute to the greatest of the great, Félix Leclerc.'

He began to play to a brisk rhythm. Before long my mum could not help but join in and clap her hands. Alexis sang the first verse.

'I found my joy by the side of the road
It looked pretty sad so I gave it a ride . . .'

As she gazed at Boris, Julie began to cry, but there was something joyful about her tears. Alexis was looking at Simon and Michel, holding hands.

'My brothers all forgot me, I fell down, I feel so bad!
If you don't pick me up, I'll surely die, this song's so sad!'

The two men were visibly moved. Then Alexis stared at Simon alone, slowing the tempo.

'Kind sir, I beg you, release me from my pain . . .'

I felt a hand on my shoulder.

'Follow me. I've got to talk to you.'

I went with Alex into the bedroom. Pipo, no doubt in a state of shock at finding so many people in his house, was peeking out from under the bed.

'I'm sorry about yesterday. I just didn't want it to end.'

He looked me right in the eye. He was waiting

for me to forgive him. I smiled. He went over to the bed and reached under the pillow for a record in its sleeve, then handed it to me.

'That's my mother.'

I felt my throat tighten, I couldn't help it.

'She's really pretty.'

'Now I know why I don't look like my dad.'

'It's because you look like your mum.'

'No, it's mainly because he's not my real dad.'

I had to sit down on the bed. I looked at Alex, and I didn't know what to say. He was so calm, almost like a grown-up. He sat next to me. We were both looking at the record sleeve.

'But Alexis is my dad, my only dad. My mum's name is Dorores. Dorores Sanchez. She lives in Mexico . . .'

Alex had his own story at last.

'My dad fell in love with her at first sight. He didn't know she was already pregnant with me. She didn't know, either. She was a good singer, and he wanted to give her the most beautiful present on earth . . . He's the one who paid for the recording, with his own money. He did everything; she just sang what he told her to sing. He wanted to make her a star.'

I looked at the sleeve. Al and Doro. I'd never heard of them. If someone's a star, even if it was a long time ago, your parents tell you about them. Alex put his hand in the sleeve and pulled out a tiny newspaper clipping.

'Read this—you'll understand.'

I read out loud.

'"I Got You Babe" by Sonny and Cher is a pop classic. This disco version of it—in French!—completely bombs. "Je t'ai bébé" is a classic failure,

168

courtesy of the insipid Al and the woman we hope never to hear again, Doro.'

In the sitting room, Alexis was singing even louder.

'My happiness left without taking my hand.'

'She *was* forgotten. She was so ashamed, and so mad at my dad. She came here to live out her dreams, and it ended up being a nightmare. But to give me a better life than I would have had in Mexico, she left me with Alexis. He wasn't really up to it . . .'

'I thought I might die of sorrow and longing.'

'That's why he became what he is . . . or rather, was. Simon told him he had blocked his emotions, that it was as if the clock had stopped for him, and that's why he was angry with everyone. But these past three days he's been able to talk about it at last—and it's like finding a whole new dad . . .'

'And where is your mother?'

'I don't know. In heaven, in Mexico . . . It doesn't matter.'

He could see that I didn't understand.

'The main thing is that now I know I've *got* a mother. You won't understand, you've always had one.'

It was true. I may have been mad at my mum, but to be angry with a mother, you have to have one to start with. You always want more, even though you haven't really appreciated what you've already got. Alex turned to me and suddenly gave me a big hug, squeezing me very tight.

'Thanks for doing all this for me.'

Was this really big tough Alex—the terror of the school—who was crying in front of me?

'I'd like to listen to the record.'

169

'Really?'

'Yes, why wouldn't I?'

'In spite of what you read?'

'But they're still your mum and dad. You don't have to be ashamed of them.'

When we went into the sitting room, Alexis had put down his guitar and was having a drink. My mum's cheeks were a little pink, but she didn't say no when she was offered more wine. Simon was with my dad, who had managed to wedge a glass into his cast-bound fingers.

'Tell me, Martin, what did you mean by a "lazybones policeman"?'

'Well, it's not as if I was in the thick of the action . . .'

When Simon saw Alex heading for the stereo with the record in his hand, he nudged Michel. There was a sudden heavy silence, because Alexis had stopped talking, too. There were still tears on Alex's cheeks. When Alexis saw the record sleeve he stood up. Simon didn't let him get very far.

'Alexis, if he wants us to hear the song, you have to let him.'

Alexis sat down again at once. It was weird, like Simon had become his boss. Alex put the record on the turntable. He turned around and gave us all a defiant look. When the disco beat started, Julie stood up at once.

'Wow, listen to that rhythm!'

She climbed onto the coffee table and began to dance—well, let's say undulate.

'Julie, maybe the table isn't the best place?'

'Sorry! But I don't know how to dance anywhere else!'

I thought it was really lovely, the way she was

dancing. Boris too thought it was really lovely. And so did my dad, I could tell he thought it was really lovely. Especially as Julie was turning around and looking at each of the men in turn. My mum didn't like it as much.

'All we need is for her to start undressing.'

When Julie took her sweater off, Simon went to talk to her. But since the music was really loud, he had to shout, so everyone heard.

'Time to calm down now, Julie! There are children here!'

I could tell my dad was sort of disappointed. He caught me looking at him and he winked. Simon began to dance. For a guy he was a really good dancer. He took Michel's hand and they wiggled their hips together.

'Come on, everybody dance now!'

Boris got up on the coffee table to join Julie. She was waving her arms and he started to do the same. But he really wasn't any good. My dad was still looking at Julie. It annoyed my mum, and she stood up.

'Right, let's dance!'

'It's been ages since we danced together!'

To remind herself of the way things used to be, my mum drained the glass of wine someone had just handed to her. She was a good dancer, my mum. Now my dad looked only at her. He was waving his casts rhythmically. Alexis stood behind Alex and put his hands on his shoulders.

'You see how they like it?'

They looked proudly at everyone dancing. Alex didn't stop crying, all the way through.

Je t'ai bébééééééé . . .

My mum was out of breath, hanging onto my

dad. Julie let herself fall backwards: she trusted
Boris. He put out his arms, ready to catch her, the
way you do at the end of a tango.

Click!

All of a sudden it was pitch dark. And then we
heard Julie falling off the coffee table. Boris hadn't
caught her. *Thud!*

'*Golubchik?* Are you all right?'

He really sounded worried. Then we heard some
weird little noises. I couldn't figure out what they
were. Then I got it: kisses!

'My Boris . . .'

'*Golubchik* . . .'

Then some more kisses, more and more.

'Calm down, Julie!'

Scratch! Michel struck a match and quickly lit
some candles, putting out the fire that Julie had
started. With the glow of light, my mum stepped
back from my dad. Julie got to her feet, adjusting
her skirt. And Boris—he had a foolish smile on his
face. Alex came over to me.

'I'm sure he's fucked her.'

I really don't like to talk about stuff like that. It
was a weird situation. The ice storm had caught up
with us again. Fortunately, my dad took control of
things.

'Right, what do we do now?'

'Just when the party was getting going. What a
shame!'

'Alexis, don't let your newly regained happiness
blind you to the fact that there are others in the city
who are less fortunate . . .'

'Sorry, Simon.'

'We're really lucky to be able to have a party
while others are having a terrible time of it.'

Everyone felt guilty.

'The old people's home!'

It was Julie who thought of it first.

'Can you imagine them all by themselves in their rooms, alone in the dark, without television?'

'It won't last, Hydro-Québec will have it all up and running in no time.'

'Don't be so sure, Simon!'

My mum was all huddled up. She was already cold. I wasn't worried about her—far from it. If she got deep-frozen it would help her think more clearly. Up until now the sky had helped everyone else, so it was time to finish the job by taking care of me. I hoped Hydro-Québec wouldn't screw up my plan. Sometimes it's hard to stop thinking about yourself.

'Why don't we go and help them?'

'Who?'

'The old folks!'

'That's a great idea, Alexis. It's important to think about others.'

'Great. Let's get going!'

'Alexis, I meant the idea, your inner path. Let's not get carried away. There's no rush.'

We heard the siren of a fire engine in the street. Then another, and another.

'I'm going!'

'Me too!'

It seemed strange to hear my dad wanting to get back in the action.

'*Davai!*'

'Boris, let's stay together!'

'Anne, you stay with the kids!'

My dad headed towards the door without another word and my mum just laughed. Julie,

173

Boris and Michel followed him. Simon didn't seem as motivated as the others; he just stood there. There was sweat on his brow. Alexis shook him.

'Hey, come on, we need you!'

'I don't mind listening to other people's misery, but I can't stand seeing it.'

My mum seized her chance.

'Simon, that's perfectly understandable. Let me leave the kids with you.'

Simon didn't protest and he immediately sat down. My mum rushed out into the corridor. Alexis gave Simon a comforting hug, and we could hear Julie shouting in the distance.

'Boris, your fish!'

There was a heavy silence. Alex and I got up and went to see what was happening. Everyone was looking at Boris: he was trembling. Julie gave him an imploring gaze. He raised his chin, as proud as only a Russian can be.

*   *   *

'We Quebeckers stick together!'

IT'S ALL THANKS TO A NATURAL DISASTER!

The streets were cordoned off all around the old people's home, which was lit only by car headlamps and the revolving lights of the police cars. Two yellow school buses were waiting, their engines running. Firefighters, policemen, ambulance drivers and Red Cross volunteers were helping the old people to evacuate the premises, one by one.

In every society a hierarchy is formed. When a group goes into action they need a leader, either self-proclaimed or elected by his fellows. Martin strode ahead, with Alexis on his right. Anne, Boris, Michel and Julie followed, in no particular order.

Just off to one side was Staff Sergeant Couillard, in charge of the evacuation. Without a moment's hesitation, Martin planted himself in front of him.

'I'm family! What can we do to help?'

'What do you mean, family?'

Martin lowered his voice.

'I teach at the police academy.'

'I see. Were you out in the field for long?'

'Five, six years.'

Staff Sergeant Couillard could not help but throw him a scornful little look. It was obvious. In the police, those who can, do; those who no longer can, teach. Martin was caught off guard, and he surveyed his troops, who suddenly looked doubtful. A voice bellowed from the patrol car's loudspeaker.

'Boss? Boss? You there, boss? Boss? Are you there?'

Exasperated, Staff Sergeant Couillard turned

175

from the car door he'd been leaning on and picked up the radio in his car.

'Yeah sure, I'm here, where else do you want me to be? Talk!'

'We're in the shit here, boss, it's taking fifteen minutes to get even one resident out. They cry and cling to the bars on their beds, they all want to take their knick-knacks with them . . . We need reinforcements.'

'Do what you can. We don't have any reinforcements, it's a mess everywhere! Think about the big picture before you start complaining!'

'But boss, at this rate, it will take days!'

'Let me analyse the situation. I'll see what I can do.'

'Thanks, boss!'

Staff Sergeant Couillard didn't look far. He eyed Martin from head to toe, sizing him up.

'How do you think you'll manage with those casts?'

'I'm in charge of my team and their contribution!'

The sergeant then turned to evaluate the team. Instinctively, Julie, Boris, Michel, Anne and Alexis stood to attention. This discouraged him more than anything.

'Damned ice! It's really only because I'm in the shit here. Okay, fine. You can help. I just need to check one thing.'

The chief moved closer to Martin.

'Blow!'

Martin didn't blow very hard, but it was enough for an experienced nose. Martin's troops thought this was hysterical, and began blowing on each other.

'Not one of you behind the wheel, you hear?'

'We hear!'

'You can take the fifth floor.'

When Martin turned around, Anne gave a shiver. His expression had changed. It was nothing to do with the alcohol; it was a look she had known in another life. She had thought it was lost forever, but now there it was again. It hadn't vanished, it had just faded away, and now in the middle of the ice storm it had begun to shine again.

'Anne, Julie, Michel, Alexis, Boris: above all you need to act, but before you act, you think! Got that?'

'Yes.'

'Yes, who?'

'Yes, Martin!'

'Michel, Alexis and Boris, you're in charge of carrying people. That's the part that needs muscles. Anne and Julie, you'll take care of the belongings, the wellbeing and the morale of the people we're evacuating. That's the part that needs brains. Any recalcitrant cases and you deal with them, talk to them, while the men take the folks who are ready out to the buses. I want at least one person out of there every five minutes. We have to act quickly, but we have to use our heads, too. Is that clear?'

'Yes, Martin!'

'Follow me!'

Staff Sergeant Couillard watched as the strange little troupe headed into the building. Puzzled, he rubbed his cap, then picked up his radio again.

'What are you doing up there, for it to take you fifteen minutes to get one person out? What did they teach you over at the police academy? Do I have to

177

explain everything?'

'Go on, one more time!'

'Monsieur Archambault, other people are waiting their turn.'

'I haven't laughed this much in fifteen years.'

'Okay, okay, but this is the last time. Show some solidarity, Monsieur Archambault.'

'I promise to show some solidarity . . . afterwards.'

Alexis spun the wheelchair over the ice. The beaming octogenarian was in no hurry, recovering from his fit of giggles. But elderly people are not necessarily kind-hearted towards each other, and promises of solidarity can quickly be forgotten.

'Don't do it with old Tremblay. He's always bugging us in the cafeteria.'

When Monsieur Archambault was finally lifted onto the yellow bus, already full of people, he was greeted with a round of applause. Followed by a heated debate.

'I'll bet that the next ones out will be the Gagné twins. Two bucks at three to one! Who'll wager?'

'I'm in!'

'Archambault! Stop betting all your money, otherwise there'll be nothing left for your heirs.'

A new peal of laughter rippled through the bus. From the windows, thirty or so pensioners with smiling faces waited for the next one to come out. After a minute or so Julie and Anne appeared, leading two perfectly identical seventy-year-old gentlemen by the arm.

'Those twins have a way with pretty women, now,

178

don't they.'

'You owe me two bucks.'

On the bus, a new round of applause greeted the arrival of the Gagné brothers. And the singing began:

'Oh they're just like us, joining us here on the bus.'

In the general cheer, no one had noticed Boris gingerly assisting an old lady to the door of the bus. She clung to his neck and hugged him for a long while, while Anne and Julie looked on, clearly moved.

'Will you come and visit us, Boris?'

'We're neighbours! I'll stop by with my girlfriend.'

'You have a girlfriend?'

'Yes, a life partner.'

Julie collapsed into Anne's arms. Boris helped the old lady up the steps onto the bus. Martin came out of the building and went over to Staff Sergeant Couillard, who was sprawled against his patrol car: the entire fifth floor had been cleared, whereas Couillard's own men had only evacuated half of the second floor.

'Mission accomplished!'

'I know, I know . . .'

'What shall we do now?'

'What would you do in my place?'

'I'd ask me to clear the fourth floor.'

'That's it . . . That's it . . . Clear the fourth floor.'

With a snap of his fingers Martin rounded up his troops. Just as he was about to go to the rescue of the fourth floor the staff sergeant sidled up to him so no one else could hear.

'How did you do it? We haven't even done half a floor.'

179

'Downplay it, explain, act positive, organise! And then . . . act!'

'Oh right, I remember now, it was in the course . . . But tell me, how do you do it, how do you get that *esprit de corps* into your team?'

Martin looked at the cast on his arm—his watch, that is.

'Staff Sergeant, I'm sorry, but I have a whole floor to clear and I don't want to get to bed too late. We can talk about it some other time if you like?'

'Sorry. Do what you need to do. I won't bother you.'

Martin turned round to count his team to make sure everyone was there. Anne suddenly realised that she would have liked to have been more than just a number; she would so have liked to be number one, the only one following her man into this new adventure.

'He's quite a man, your husband,' said Julie.

'I don't know what's happening to me.'

'I feel the same, but whatever it is, I'm embracing it with open arms.'

'How long have you known Boris?'

'Three days, since the start of this stupid ice storm. Well, I say stupid, but if it weren't for the ice storm I wouldn't have got to know him. That's what's crazy. Basically, I've got a natural disaster to thank!'

Anne looked at Julie for a long time before raising her eyes to the sky. Then looked down at the ground covered in ice. Finally she turned to Martin: ramrod straight like a policeman, he was bravely leading his team of ad hoc rescue workers into their next mission. She fell in, looping her arm round Julie's elbow, and put her head on her new friend's shoulder.

'You're right, Julie, my love. It's all thanks to a natural disaster.'

Friday, 9 January 1998

'The situation is reaching crisis point. In five days up to a hundred millimetres of ice have fallen in the "black triangle" between Saint-Hyacinthe, Saint-Jean-sur-le-Richelieu and Granby. In Montérégie, up to eighty millimetres of ice have fallen. While Montreal has not had to deal with such a heavy ice fall, the situation remains critical this morning, since four out of the five power lines supplying Montreal are out of service. Once again, on this "black Friday", we are nearing a total blackout for the entire city . . .'

'As if by some miracle, the freezing rain stopped at the end of the afternoon . . .'

I DIDN'T PUT ANY MORE LOGS ON THE FIRE

I always wake up at night because I have to go for a wee.

When I opened my eyes, at first I didn't know where I was. I was in the sitting room in my own house, but I had fallen asleep on the sofa at Simon and Michel's place. I was on a mattress, my parents'. There was an orange light flickering, coming from the fireplace. There was whispering. I looked up. My dad was drying his casts above the flames, my mum was sitting next to him. I closed my eyes again, but not my ears. At last they were talking about me.

'He asked some strange questions when you weren't here.'

'What sort of questions?'

'How did we first meet? He asked me that the day you left.'

'Do you remember how we met?'

'I think so.'

'The way you felt, and why you liked me?'

'Three days ago I didn't really remember. But I admit, you refreshed my memory tonight.'

'I thought about it a lot at the cottage. About how you forget things or don't see them any more, about how you change. I wanted to find those insignificant little things that made us want to live together, that made us love each other. I thought that if everything had to come to an end, I had to remember what had brought us together in the first place, rather than make lists of everything that had started keeping us apart.'

'Do you realise that if it weren't for this ice you wouldn't even be thinking like that right now?'

'It's because we've temporarily lost our routine, and all our bad habits, the ones that keep you from seeing, that make you passive. After a while you have to try to remember who you were. I tell you, being cold refreshed my memory.'

The virtues of being deep-frozen!

'One night he burst into tears and told me he thought it was his fault.'

'What did you say to him?'

'That it wasn't his fault at all, of course. That it was a thing between adults.'

'I'm not even sure any more.'

'What do you mean?'

'He was presented with a *fait accompli*—no one asked him his opinion. It can't be easy, not for a little fellow who's only eleven.'

At last they were beginning to get it. But my dad, who'd been deep-frozen for longer, was still way ahead of my mum.

'It's as if we jumped on the separation solution right away, because it's the easiest, it's what everyone does, and you never stop to wonder if you've really tried everything.'

'This is too emotional for me. Three days ago I thought you'd be walking out of here with that armchair stuck to your bottom, because you never seemed to get out of it. You come back with both arms in a cast. All you can think of is joking around. Then you manage to evacuate a hundred old people, and the staff sergeant wanted you to explain the rescue operation to the press, rather

186

than do it himself. And now you're telling me things I never thought I'd ever hear you say, let alone think. I need some sleep. I need to think . . .'

I slipped my hand out from under the sheet. It was cold. The situation was improving, but I hadn't asked the sky to stop yet. The ice had to finish the job at our place, too. It might be selfish of me, but I thought that we needed the help at our place more than anywhere. I was happy for Alex, but I wanted to be happy, too. I decided not to go for a wee. I held it in and thought as hard as I could about the three of us. I must have fallen asleep really fast.

*   *   *

At ten o'clock the light in the hallway woke me up. It was still cold. I was worried—the power had come back on so quickly. Why did they have to reconnect my building when there were millions of other people who had no power? Hydro-Québec were determined to give me a hard time.

My dad must have been very tired because he was snoring really loudly. I got up slowly. I waited before I looked at him; I was afraid he'd be alone. I took a deep breath and turned my head. I wish I'd had my video camera. Mum and Dad were holding each other so close, as if they were one person. They were cold.

*   *   *

I didn't put any more logs on the fire.

187

IS THERE ANYTHING MORE BEAUTIFUL THAN LOVE?

'Nineteen!'

'And at the other end?'

'Nineteen!'

'Julie! Wait for the thermometer to settle.'

Julie, in a red nightie, raised her eyes to the ceiling. She did not think of protesting, not even for a second. She dipped the thermometer into the other end of the aquarium. Across from her Boris was whistling, light-hearted, and Brutus was sitting on his lap. She had heard her fair share of men whistling after lovemaking, but this sweet melody didn't sound like the others. At the height of ecstasy, Boris had moaned:

'Ya lyublyu tebya . . .'

Four times she had heard that cry from the heart, which needed no dictionary. She too had moaned, with the sublime feelings that had run through her:

'I love you! I love you! I love you!'

The two cats had always considered the sofa their territory—and an ideal springboard to the aquarium—but now they beat a hasty retreat when Brutus delivered a vicious swipe to the larger of the two. Julie smiled. Ever since he had grown attached to Boris, Brutus had been gaining in self-confidence, and would not tolerate either of his fellows going anywhere near the aquarium. Julie thought very hard about love. With the thermometer in the water, she recalled what her mother had said, the mother whom she had left when she was so young.

Sometimes you need to let time do its work before you can understand what your parents were trying to teach you.

'You'll see, my dear, when you make love to a man you really love, the pleasure is different. It's unique, because the heart makes it so much more powerful.'

Julie looked at her whistling Boris, who had just taken out his sheets of paper with his calculations on again. Her mother was right: last night she had finally felt what she had been waiting for for so long. In the past, she had known many imperfect loves. Now the present was perfect, pluperfect, and at last she could imagine a future.

'Boris, the thermometer still says nineteen!'

He put the sheets detailing the trajectories of each fish down on the coffee table. Well, the earlier trajectories, at thirty-two degrees.

'*Golubchik?* Did you observe their new behaviour?'

In spite of her intense desire to understand Boris's experiments and to share the effort that went into them, for all her three days' experience in topology Julie had to confess she was still very much a novice.

'It's not easy, with the thermometer.'

'*Milaya*, look. Look carefully . . .'

'Can I take the thermometer out of the water?'

'Yes, yes, of course.'

Julie watched the fish. Just above the surface of the water, Boris was tracing Number Two's path with his finger. With his other hand, he was following Number Four. Julie cheated a little. She just watched her man's fingers as they performed their ballet.

189

'They're not following the same path any more!'

'Exactly!'

Boris stared at Julie.

'It's obvious! Fish change direction in cold weather!'

Julie was pleased with her answer. It was so pleasant to be able to have these early morning exchanges with her learned Russian lover. But even after lovemaking, a mathematician who is a candidate for the most magnificent of PhDs cannot help but make you feel that you are a long way from knowing as much as he does.

'Look, *golubchik*, you're missing something very obvious.'

Julie was a little disappointed, especially as Boris did not let the matter drop.

'Take a good look—it's striking.'

Boris could not grasp that topology, as expressed by the hermetic language of pure mathematics, especially first thing in the morning, was anything but obvious to the rest of the world. But Julie wanted to share everything with him. She concentrated hard, searching for the obvious thing in the water. Suddenly she found it.

'They're following a new path!'

Boris nodded. 'Yes, indeed . . . I am going to study their new trajectories at nineteen degrees and compare them with the ones at thirty-two. It should only delay my dissertation by a year or two. We'll see what comes of it. Despite my misfortune, I am lucky they did not die.'

Boris got up and gave a long sigh of disappointment at the thought that he would have to start his calculations all over again. But Julie the researcher had not finished.

190

'It looks as if they're swimming closer to each other.'

Boris quickly sat back down by the aquarium. Julie still had something to say.

'That's it! When it's cold, they get closer to each other.'

Boris opened his big blue eyes. Across from him, Julie took a deep breath. Her eyes were sparkling.

'And they're swimming two by two, in pairs. They're no longer plotting their course individually, avoiding the others. They're doing it together. And it's just since they got cold that they've been like this. Look! Now they're making double knots.'

Boris had never envisaged such a sophisticated topological conclusion. He leaned over the aquarium for a closer verification of his lovely Julie's theory. Number Two could not stop rubbing his right fin against the rear scales of Number Three. As for Number One, it came out from behind the little rockery with what looked like a silly grin on its face—a phenomenon rarely observed in exotic fish in captivity—followed by Number Four, who gave a little flick of his rear fin, as if to adjust it, blowing bubbles all the while.

'Da . . . Da . . . Da.'

Boris Bogdanov studied the woman beside him: not only did she fill his heart, but she had also just found a conclusion for a basic mathematical proof, easily demonstrable even by the kind of maths student who repeats his first year, and yet he, Boris, had missed it altogether. When you are in love, you are as one. Filled with wonder, he stared at his lover.

'Don't you think, Julie, that this is a little like the fabulous discoveries by Pierre and Marie Curie?'

Julie racked her brains, going way back in time, but couldn't find it.

'I saw the film, when I was little. We'll have to rent it.'

That was what Boris loved about Julie. She was natural, honest and logical. And she had soft skin, firm breasts, the body of a goddess and a torrid sensuality, not to mention the fact that she was divinely good at kissing. Early in the morning the path between extreme mathematical thought and sudden desire of the most animal kind is much shorter than one might suppose, particularly for a researcher who has just found what he was looking for.

'*Golubchik*, come to the bedroom!'

*   *   *

'Morning, lover boys!'

Alexis had entered the room without knocking. He was holding a tray. On it were two plates with bacon omelettes, two glasses of orange juice, four slices of toast and two piping hot strong coffees. Simon could scarcely hide his emotion. He turned to Michel who was still sleeping against his shoulder.

'Wake up, my love. Look at the yummy breakfast Alexis has made for us.'

Just four days earlier these two had hardly dared leave the house in each other's company, and now they were being served a lovely breakfast by the neighbour from across the street—a man whom they had known for only three days.

'Sit up, lover boys, otherwise it'll get cold!'

Just as Alexis was about to set the tray down on

192

the bed, Simon grabbed his arm.

'How can we thank you, Alexis . . .'

'Oh, it's nothing, just two little eggs and—'

'That's not what I mean. I mean for seeing us the way you do.'

'Well, it's mostly thanks to you. No, it's totally thanks to you. It has done me good to talk to you. Thank you! Thanks to both of you.'

'Don't thank us; you've all helped us as much as we've helped you. Before we met you we were different. Now, because of you, so much has changed, and our life will never be the same. You'll come to our wedding! Well, that is, the day the law allows it.'

'Well, I must say for a couple that's not married, you made one hell of a noise last night.'

'Alexis, we don't speak Russian when we make love.'

'It was Boris?'

'Yes, and he didn't stop all night! Four times! I couldn't sleep a wink.'

Alex was walking by in the hallway, followed by Pipo. The two had become inseparable.

'Told you, Dad, told you it was them!'

'I see you've been expanding the range of your topics of conversation. That's very good, very constructive. But there might be other subjects you could discuss with your son . . .'

'At that age they're curious, it's normal. Besides, let me tell you, Simon, I can understand that Boris. When you've got a bike as gorgeous as that, you want to ride it all the time!' Alexis couldn't help but wink at his two friends. 'Don't you think?'

'That's one way of seeing things.'

'Right, okay, I'll let you eat, it's going to get

193

cold.'

Alexis took his son by the shoulder, with a warm protective gesture, the kind only a true dad knows how to make.

'Want to take Pipo for a walk?'

The bedroom door closed gently. Simon and Michel looked at each other with an air of complicity. They picked up their toast to butter it. But before biting into it they exchanged a gentle kiss. And immediately made a face—from the other side of the wall came a loud banging.

'Oh, no! Are they at it again?'

The tempo suddenly increased. A very loud banging on the walls. Not until the toast was already cold did deliverance come.

'Aaaaaahhhhh! *Ya lyublyu tebya!*'

'I love you . . . aaah! I love you . . . aaah! I love you . . . aaah!'

And silence returned. Simon bit into his stone-cold toast. He chewed it gingerly. As soon as he had swallowed it, he turned to Michel.

*   *   *

'Is there anything more beautiful than love?'

ALL'S WELL THAT ENDS WELL

A lot of people like to do their thinking in the shower. My mum and dad must have been getting twice as much thinking done, since they were in there together.

When they woke up at around one o'clock in the afternoon, they couldn't see me. I was hidden. And I was afraid: it was warm in the house. Still lying on the mattress in the sitting room, they disentangled themselves before they looked at each other sheepishly. Neither one wanted to be the first to speak. They gazed at each other, surprised to find themselves like that. My mum said the first thing that came into her nose.

'Smells like a policeman who's been working hard all night!'

When they came upon me in the hallway, the two of them covered me with affectionate kisses. But this time my mum didn't ask me to help my dad get washed. Maybe she didn't have time. They looked like they were really in a hurry. I wouldn't have listened to them if they hadn't been talking so loudly. No, that's not true. I would have listened.

'Stop moving like that, I'll take it off for you myself!'

'If I stay on one leg I'll fall over.'

'Hold on to me. I said, "hold on", not "rub up against me"!'

'It's because of the casts.'

'Raise your other leg so I can take off your boxer shorts.'

'Okay, okay . . . There, it's raised.'

195

'Oh, you pig!'

I don't know if they were doing a lot of thinking, but they were certainly making some funny noises.

'Oohhhh!'

'Aahhhh!'

My mum went along with everything now.

'Oh yes! Oh yes! Oh yes!'

Sometimes there are things you understand but you don't want to admit that you do. I knew what my mum and dad were doing in the shower. Even if it made me happy, I don't want to talk about it. They didn't want to talk about it either when they came out of the bathroom. They walked past me, whistling. The phone rang and I picked it up. I didn't want to stop the music.

'Staff Sergeant Couillard here. May I speak to Martin? It's urgent!'

*   *   *

When we got to the old people's home with my mum and dad, the evacuees for a night were climbing out of the school buses. They seemed glad to be coming home. As soon as they saw my dad they all stood around him and cheered. Dad had become the old folks' hero. I stuck right by him, so I heard what Staff Sergeant Couillard had to say.

'They wouldn't come home until you got here!'

My dad got loads of kisses. All the old people wanted to touch him and thank him and hug him.

'Careful, Archambault, you're going to break his casts!'

'Didn't I already shake your hand?'

'That was my twin.'

'Hey, you Gagné lot, let the others have their

196

turn!'

'I'll bet you two bucks that he lives less than a block away.'

'You're on.'

My dad had to promise he'd come again before they finally agreed to go back to their rooms. I was so proud of him. I think Mum was even prouder than I was. I caught a glimpse of her gazing at him admiringly; she was laughing, she was happy. I liked that Staff Sergeant Couillard. I could tell that he liked my dad, too.

'I don't see why you don't come back to the force. A guy of your calibre, you're not meant to be vegetating at the police academy.'

My mum crossed her fingers and closed her eyes. Her wish had been fulfilled. My dad didn't say anything, but you could see his answer in his eyes. Mum was glued to his side. He turned to her and they looked at each other for a long time. They moved closer together—well, their lips did, especially; they were already pretty close. They kissed for a very, very long time. This time it really was like in the movies. Even Staff Sergeant Couillard had to wipe away a tear, it was that beautiful. I didn't close my eyes; I didn't want to miss a single moment. I waited for the words 'The End' to appear in front of me, like in the movies. I'd recorded the scene in my head. I'd be able to play it back my whole life long.

*   *   *

The moment we went into the sitting room, Dad settled into his armchair. Mum immediately joined him, sitting on the armrest. She put her hand on his shoulder, just like in the old days. I watched them. I didn't say anything. It was funny, the way they were looking at each other questioningly to decide who would be the first to speak. I wasn't in a hurry. A few minutes more or a few less, it doesn't really matter when it's forever. This time I wanted to hear what I knew they were going to say. No one at school had ever told me this story. I wanted to enjoy every second.

'We've been thinking . . .'

'Maybe we were a bit too hasty making our decision . . .'

'We realise we still love each other very much, and there are bound to be lots of things we can experience together . . .'

'So, we don't want to split up any more.'

'Everything will go back to the way it was.'

'Not the way it was . . . even better.'

I could tell they were waiting for me to say something. I didn't know whether I should tell them that I might have had something to do with their 'thinking'. But I wanted to let them have the last word—they were my parents, after all. They looked at each other as if they knew they'd had a really close call.

'It looks like we owe the heavens one. If it weren't for this ice storm . . . Can you imagine, my love?'

*   *   *

In my bedroom, I felt glad I hadn't told them my secret. What would be the point? I lay on my back in my bed. I looked up at the ceiling. It was white, but white the way it used to be. They weren't going

198

to be splitting me between them; I wasn't going to be the fourteenth kid in my class to have to migrate every week; and all three of us would be going back to the summer cottage, together.

I turned to the window but I couldn't see the sky from my bed. So I got up: I had to tell it to its face. I looked up and it was all white. It lit up the ground still covered in ice. I couldn't get over what it had done for me. I stayed there with the sky for a long time, trying to find a way to say goodbye. I didn't want to muddle up my words. I hope I didn't disappoint it.

'Hey, thanks for listening to me.'

*   *   *

When I went back into the sitting room the television was on, but my parents weren't there. I was about to go and switch it off but just then the weather map appeared on the news channel. Even if the sky had never let me down, I wanted to make sure it had really heard me. I couldn't help but smile. It looked like the sky could never do things by halves.

'The forecast for tomorrow, Saturday, is sunshine and blue sky for the entire Montreal region. Our experts at Météo Canada are categorical: no more freezing rain. The storm of the century is really over.'

Click! I switched off the television and went to look for my parents. They were in the little study. Dad was finishing his letter of resignation to the police academy. Mum was looking over his shoulder and seemed to be savouring every word that lit up the computer screen. Once they'd printed the letter, my dad signed it, folded it and put it in the envelope that my mum held out to him, already with its stamp on. He got up and gave me a smile.

'You coming with us to post it?'

'Oh, yes!'

We went out into the hallway to put on our coats. While my mum was helping him, my dad gave me a big smile of complicity.

'Frankly, if I were you, I'd grab this opportunity to film the street. You're not likely to witness another natural disaster like this one in your lifetime. I for one have never seen a storm like it!'

'Dad's right, it would be a pity not to use the present he gave you . . . well, that we gave you for Christmas.'

'I'm not in the mood.'

I don't know whether it was because he'd written his letter about returning to active police duty, but I was dead sure he'd already got his policeman's instinct back. It must have been written all over my face that I was lying.

'Let me have a look at your video camera.'

I mustn't spoil the most beautiful day of my life. I had to tell the truth.

'*What?* In the educational director's office? Didn't I tell you not to take it to school?'

It wasn't mean, the way my dad spoke to me. I answered from the heart.

'We all make mistakes.'

My parents looked at each other. I could tell they felt foolish. Dad immediately took me in his arms. I could feel a hand in my hair and I could tell right away that it was Mum's: there was no cast.

'You're right. Life will always give you a second chance.'

School started again on Monday morning. Alex was waiting for me as usual at the bottom of the stairs to my building. He could see right away that I was anxious. He looked at me with a little smile and gave me a friendly pat on the shoulder. Without a word he opened his schoolbag, took out an envelope and handed it to me.

'What's this?'

'Julie wrote it.'

'Why'd she write a letter?'

'About the video camera.'

'Did you tell her I'd filmed her?'

'Don't worry, she's really nice. And she's in love now, anyway, so she's even nicer.'

'What does she say in the letter?'

'That we were making a film about the story of a little lost cat, and when we were filming we didn't notice that you could see her breasts . . .'

'The educational director will never believe it.'

*   *   *

It wasn't that she didn't believe it: she couldn't care less. She was on the phone when we went into her office. She didn't even look at us. She was standing up, and there was a huge cushion on her chair.

'He fell on his coccyx, too! It's incredible, the ambulance stopped to pick him up on the way. We went up to radiology at the same time. We both broke our coccyxes in the exact same place! We were lying on our stretchers, and it was love at first sight. Can you imagine how lucky that was? Ten

201

years I've been looking for love!'

Alex looked at me. His admiration for all my good works was boundless.

'Hang on a second, I have someone in my office . . . Why are you two here, anyway?'

'For my video camera, Miss . . .'

'Oh right, I remember. Don't do it again.'

She opened her drawer. She definitely didn't feel like talking to us. She handed the video camera to me but she was looking at Alex. Even he was surprised when she spoke to him in a really kind way.

'Your father left a message. He wants to come and see me to discuss how things are going for you at school. That's very good news. Work hard and I'll have nothing but nice things to tell him.'

*   *   *

We didn't talk on the way home. It was as if we needed to digest it all. Alex couldn't wipe the little smile off his face. I think we were doing the same thing, in silence. We were looking at all the people passing us in the street and wondering if something had changed in their lives.

When we got to the top of our road we could see Michel and Simon in the distance walking Pipo together. We sat down on the steps by Alex's front door. Then we heard someone whistle. It was no surprise to see Boris, his hair all dishevelled, come out on Julie's arm. She turned to us. Alex just gave her a thumbs up, and Julie winked at him. They disappeared around the corner. I stood up.

'I'm going home, my parents are waiting for me.'

'Me too. My dad found my mother's number in

202

Mexico. We're going to call her tonight.'

We looked at each other for a long time. I was really happy for him. He came up and gave me a big strong hug, and I did the same.

'Good luck, Alex.'

*   *   *

I went into the house with my video camera, and found my mum and dad in the sitting room. The television was switched off and they were sitting next to each other on the three-thousand-dollar sofa. My dad's arm was around my mum's shoulder. They both turned to look at me at the same time. I don't even remember who it was who spoke.

*   *   *

'You see? All's well that ends well.'

Nine years later

'Roll over!'

Pipo slowly does as he's told, with his tired body. He has always been a white dog, but now he has new white hairs. He is really very white, almost transparent. I know he'll only roll over once. As loyal as they come, until his dying day, he'll do his little trick to make me happy. Dogs are like great champions—you mustn't get attached to them, otherwise when you see how they're all done in at the end of their career, it will make you sad.

'Snap your fingers! Make him crawl!'

'No, he's too old now.'

'I want you to make him crawl, I said!'

When you're twenty you have your whole life ahead of you. But always trailing along behind you there is your little sister.

'I want you to make him crawl, I said!'

If my sister, at the age of nine, is a right little horror, it's because she is the baby of the family. But that isn't the only reason. My parents named her Aqua. At the register office, the registrar warned them that a name that's too original can be hard on a child, and can be a burden in the long run.

'But that was the moment her life began! We can hardly call her "In-the-Shower", can we?'

Rumour has it that a lot of children were conceived during the ice storm. They even wrote about it in the newspaper. But when your name is Aqua, it does make life tough. I may have already mentioned that children are cruel to one another.

'Aqua . . . duct? Aqua . . . lung?'

Pipo had his usual ritual wee on the little tree

that had bent double under the ice. It's grown up to be a handsome maple tree, not yet the tallest in the street, but a fine upstanding one, its top aiming proudly for the sky.

'I told you, I want you to make him crawl!'

'He's too old. Simon and Michel don't want us to tire him out.'

'They don't need to know. It'll be our secret!'

          *   *   *

Michel and Simon never again bought Chivas Royal Salute 21 Year Old. They even decided never to drink it again. Those moments they had thought were special had concealed nothing more than a desire not to exist.

When Simon went to speak to the president of the Quebec psychologists' association, it was with his head on a platter, for he reasoned that if he cut it off right from the start it wouldn't hurt as much. But even when you think you're done for, there are truths in life just waiting to catch up with you.

'Simon, it's hardly important. Look at me. I have a big belly and not a hair on my head! Where do you think I met Sonia? She's twenty-three years younger than I am! Have you taken a good look at me? Do you see what a heart-throb I am?'

At Météo Canada, the revelation that Michel was gay did not cause any storms; if anything, there was a thaw. Now everyone knew. A revelation is not just an inner light, it's a glow which illuminates the true face you show the world, and it ends up changing what the world sees.

          *   *   *

'Why don't you want to make him crawl?'

Was I like this when I was little? Did people have to say the same thing twenty-five times until I finally got it?

I pulled gently on Pipo's lead so we could finish our walk around the block. He followed, taking tiny little steps. My mobile rang. They were calling me from home.

'Staff Sergeant Dad here! The twins have just arrived!'

'Pipo, time to go home.'

'I want you to make him crawl.'

'Shut up and get a move on!'

*   *   *

On that fateful 9 January 1998, when my mother and father told me that they were not going to split up after all, I was not able to savour my joy for long.

'Alexandria! Alexandra!'

Julien and the twins had been without power for three days. They lived in Montérégie, a region that had been hit hard by the ice storm. So there was a price to be paid for happiness regained. It was as if the sky were sending me the bill.

The sirens in the port of Alexandria
Still sing the same melody . . . wow wow . . .

The twins ran all over the place and jumped on anything that might be remotely bouncy. They barged into my bedroom without knocking and wanted me to play with them no matter what. This vision of hell lasted three whole weeks until, finally, they went home.

But the virtue of time is that it enables plants

209

to grow, even the ones you thought you were allergic to. If they become beautiful and bloom with lovely petals, you don't look at them the same way. Nowadays Alexandria and Alexandra have transformed their melody into a siren song.

'Go on, sweetie-pie, tell us, which one of us has nicer boobs?'

Now I feel totally at ease with the subject, and I can claim a certain amount of experience. We often talk about it with Alex. We have spent every summer for the last eight years in Mexico, in his little white house with the lovely name, *La Pequeña Felicidad*, The Little Happiness.

*   *   *

That day when I got my video camera back, after we said goodbye on the stairway, Alex went to join his dad, who was waiting for him with the telephone on his lap. Alexis unfolded a ragged little piece of paper with Dorores's phone number on it. He hesitated for a long time, for fear she might have forgotten him. But even a thousand years later you remember a voice you have loved. All she had to do was pick up the receiver.

'Hello?'

'Dorores! It's me, Alexis!'

'*¿Me perdóna tu, mi amor?*'

Thanks to Simon's ice therapy, Alexis had forgiven himself and no longer held any grudges towards anyone, least of all Dorores. He went from one construction site to the next, and sang of love and hope on the pavements of Old Montreal, and eventually he was able to buy two single tickets to Cancún. Alexis and Alex took off for Mexico in early June 1998, four weeks before the end of the year. The educational director didn't object to Alex missing the last month of school: he'd turned into a star pupil. But it had really got her down, even though she'd been in such good spirits ever since she got engaged to her fellow coccyx injury victim. She'd even had to tell the principal.

'We'll have to cancel the party in the cafeteria that we'd planned for after the final round of *Blooming Geniuses*. Without Alex, the school has no hope of winning.'

The world needs its outsiders, its dark horses who end up making it first across the finish line, otherwise hope would never be anything more than one never-ending race.

* * *

'I told you, I want you to make him crawl!'

I ran up the stairs to my apartment four at a time, with my sister at my heels and Pipo in my arms, a little dog who was only too happy not to have to subject his four skinny little paws to any further exertion.

'I'll tell Mummy that you were mean to me!'

'You do that. But you won't be able to play on the computer with Olga.'

Olga is Aqua's best friend. It's no coincidence; the sky certainly ordained it. They were born on the same day, almost at the same time, at the Sainte-Justine Hospital. Olga never makes fun of my sister's name. Only once, when they were fighting over a Russian doll, did she try.

'Aqua . . . rium!'

Although my sister forgave Olga fairly quickly,

211

Boris was hurt.

'Olga! You must not make fun of Daddy's PhD!'

Boris has changed a great deal since obtaining his PhD in mathematics from McGill University. Now a leading world expert on topology, he contributes regularly to *Nature*, the famous scientific journal, with the findings from his research. And the day he received the Fields medal, the highest award there is for a mathematician, he felt that at last he had found his place among his childhood heroes, those glorious figureheads of the communist regime whose path he had wanted to follow to join the dynasty of great scientists of the former Soviet empire.

'*Da . . . Da . . . Da . . .*'

He has a big office at the university, access to which is rigorously monitored by his very personal assistant, Julie. Only Brutus is allowed to go in and sit on the lap of the great scholar. Julie, her blouses always buttoned up to her chin, is very wary of his female colleagues: they may have all their prestigious academic qualifications, but she doesn't like them hanging round her beloved Boris's department.

'Mademoiselle, this is a prestigious university. I am of the opinion that your outfit is an insult to its history, and a hindrance to those who seek to perpetuate the tradition of quiet contemplation for the good of Humanity! In other words, the next time you wear such a low-cut neckline, you can read all about your future in the employment section of *La Presse*.'

*　　　*　　　*

212

We'd been sitting round the table when Julie told us that story. She had nothing to hide from her friends. She was still just as natural as ever, as if, by coming back to our neighbourhood, she felt just the way she had ten years earlier. These days she's a fine Westmount lady, living in a huge house with a lawn imported from London and maintained by a gardener who speaks only English. But she hasn't forgotten a thing, and every year she reminds me of the fact.

'You're a lucky boy that there's a statute of limitations for having filmed my boobs!'

Michel was the only one who didn't hear what she said. He preferred playing with the children. He and Simon had got married, but they'd never been able to adopt. *Dura lex, sed lex.*

Aqua and Olga were older, but now they had to share their toys with Natasha and Igor, the youngest, whose cheekbones were as prominent as his father's.

'Mummy says that Daddy scored a lot of short-handed goals!'

*   *   *

The children returned to the table screaming with joy when my mum emerged from the kitchen with an immense home-baked *galette des Rois*, still the best in the world. What had once been just a family tradition was now a pretext for all of us to gather every year at the beginning of January to commemorate the ice storm that had brought us all together. We always told the same stories, but that didn't matter. We never got tired of hearing them.

'And then I said to Boris, they're swimming two

213

by two, in pairs. They're not swimming all on their own and avoiding each other any more. They're together now that they're cold—look, now they're making double knots!'

My dad got the bean. My mum, naturally, was his queen. She put on her crown, taking care that it didn't slip. Everyone applauded, amidst peals of laughter. My parents looked at me closely for a moment. All it took was one look and we knew we were all remembering the same scene in the kitchen when they had told me the worst news ever. Mum and Dad hugged each other, smiled at me, then they kissed.

All afternoon I savoured the company of these people who seemed to love each other so very much. We met only once a year now, but we knew we were bound forever by that incredible ice storm—so incredible it could even have been downright supernatural.

*   *   *

That night in my room, after I'd shooed Aqua away from my computer, I waited for her to stop screaming outside my door so that I could finish writing this story.

The older you get, the better you understand the inner paths of your childhood, which can sometimes take you on strange journeys. You are able to analyse them, to figure out the causes, motives, destinations. And above all your memories help you to distinguish how much is true in everything that seems so unreal. But there is one thing I will never try to get to the bottom of: how could I have imagined I was the one who caused the ice storm? I

214

just didn't want my parents to split up, that's all.

I haven't told you my name. Now that we're on the last page, it really doesn't matter. I just wanted to remember that January in 1998, and everything that it inspired in me, so that my story can belong to all the children who would like to make themselves heard.

*   *   *

May all of life be this beautiful.

ACKNOWLEDGEMENTS . . .

. . . To everyone who, while I was writing, took the time to read the manuscript and share their constructive thoughts.

. . . To Titus, and all the team at the Café République in Outrement, for keeping that same table for me, along with the same chair, the same cup and the same smile.

. . . To my loved ones, because without them, all these words would have no meaning and no significance.